this was

E. A. Gundlach

ISBN-13: 978-0692297186
ISBN-10: 0692297189

DEDICATION

For Mom who gave me love and nightmares.

CONTENTS

WARDOG REFRESH

Broken dust shield rolled back, red oozed from the gash in Angel's pearly crew cut, ran down his temple over his hard carved cheek to drip off his chin. The drops froze before they struck my shield and went *tink* as they bounced off. Breathing a frosty plume, he said, "Trust me, Sir. You'll be all right. Just let go."

I snorted a laugh, dangling from his grip while I strained with the toe of my right boot to reach the crumbling ledge of the abutment even though it was plainly out of reach. The bottom of the Vallis wound through its monstrous curves like a serene snake beneath us. The shattered heating filaments of the aqueduct laid scattered across the floor of the canyon, sparkling in Mars' ochre haze.

Angel had been hit. He hadn't enough strength left to pull me up and he wasn't going to be able to hold me much longer. I hadn't quite made the end of the aqueduct before it blew. The concussion knocked me a good way forward, but if Angel hadn't had the enhanced reflexes and strength to snatch me out of flight, I would be tumbling lazily down the wall of the Vallis to rest in the basin with the all the broken concrete and steel span already there. As things were, there was no place else to go but down. For a moment, I stopped struggling and hung there from his grip, looked down, looked across the valley at the remnants of the aqueduct that ran back into the cliff side opposite us, then looked up into the cowl of his helmet at his weather beaten face. Dirt and blood brindled his cheeks. Angel smiled. I snickered. The Martian motto, 'Never say die' was emblazoned on our company patches, but we had been in enough tight spots to know there was no way out of this one alive.

"Angel, how much longer can you hold out?"

"My nanites have sutured the amputations of both legs and stopped the hemorrhaging there. However, the shrapnel wound to my abdominal aorta is severe. It was transected. I have redirected my invivo colony to repair the wound, but my nanitic volume is not sufficient to complete microsuturing in time. Circulatory failure is imminent. I have approximately seven minutes."

I hated to loose him. He had been a good drone, a good partner and, yes, a good friend. That's not as pathetic as it sounds. "Set up a mnemonic transfer."

He squinted faintly, "Why?"

"I'll take you with me."

He smiled. "No, Sir."

"What, 'No, Sir'? That's an order, Drone. I'll requisition you another body." That is, after I locate one for me. I wasn't about to ride this chunk of meat into the basin. I'll evac over the satellite signal with Angel piggy backed and transmit our patterns into the rescue buffer of the orbiting buoy. Once we're loaded, we can just sit tight until a friendly beam strobes through and pulls us out. After a few weeks of harmless oblivion Angel and me will wake up in fresh flesh, ready to come back here and kick some Terran asses.

Angel shook his head slowly, still smiling. Softly, he insisted, "No, Sir. No more refreshes. I've been doing this sort of work all my life. I was bredgineered to do it, so I've been glad to do it, but I'm done."

"And you're damned good. You've got a lot of good years left. All you need is a fresh body and some tech upgrades."

"No, Sir. Thank you, Sir. I'd like to finish things here. Now."

"But why? You can go on forever. We both can."

"Yes, Sir. But the truth is, I don't want to. I don't care if the next requisition a criminal or a saint. I won't refresh again. Live enough times and some day you might understand."

"Dammit, Angel. I'm giving you a direct order! You can not disobey!"

"Then court martial me posthumously, Sir." His smile grew. Oddly reverent, it raised my hackles. Something like kindness filled his pale eyes, then he said, "Good bye, Sir."

Angel let go of me.

Son of a bitch!

It took me a split second to orient myself, roll out of the tumble, hang out my arms and legs, spread eagling to make as much resistance as possible and stabilize my fall. I had to volt out immediately. Even on Mars, a fall from this height would kill me. Comming, my receivers crackled while I scanned for the bounce off the satellite. Precious nanoseconds ticked off in my head while my eyes monitored the approach of the orange floor of the gorge. Where's the signal? I cast again. I should have linked with it instantly.

Just then the crackle broke off. Someone's com beckoned. Fighting panic, hoping for a rescue, I opened my receivers.

(I'm sorry, Sir.)

(Angel! Get the Hell off my frequency! I'm trying to evac.)

(I can't let you do that. Don't you see? It's futile. Fighting and dying.)

(Fighting for our planet, Angel! Don't forget that. We belong here more than the Terrans.)

(They made us.)

(But we belong here. We can breathe this air. This is our planet. So, we lost this battle. We took out the aqueduct, Angel, and we'll keep taking them out until we win the-)

(The battles are won, the battles are lost, but the war is never over. We fight. We die. They fight. They die. We all believe in what we're fighting for or we don't, but we still fight. It has nothing to do with the cause. We're sheep, Sir, going to slaughter. We're cannon fodder. Someone has to stop the cycle. It's all about will. About understanding. About ... wisdom.)

This was hopeless.

(Angel! I need that satellite! Break off!)

(I'm sorry, Sir. But I can't. You'll just ...) his signal weakened.

I'm sure he was dying. I started to break away, but I wasted just enough time arguing that I couldn't initiate a satellite link now and transmit my mnemonic signature to it in time. The ground was coming up too fast. There was only one place to go. I seized the Angel's signal, lying through my gritted receivers, (Don't let me go like this, Angel.) I had no intention of dying. I'll turn the drone off, open an autosignal to the satellite, to then slam his body into stasis so it doesn't decay around the helix drive holding my pattern and wait for the satellite to pick me up. I'll wake up in the buffer, that's all. (If it's going to happen ....)

(Of course, Sir. Come ahead.)

I exploded into his neural net. It's a dirty feeling to burst into the head of dying man, even if he is just a drone. As I filled out his consciousness, I became aware of Angel's presence and the pain. We both sprawled on the ragged edge of the aqueduct, the ground freeze-burning our belly through our body armor as we watched, with failing eyes, my body strike the outcroppings of the cliff side, then bounce rock to rock with deceptive grace; the momentum choreographed by Mars's lazy gravity. When my body hit bottom, it bounced high a couple times, throwing up rusty-dusty plumes. I turned my attention inward to the Angel's invivo monitor. It kept a running tally of his falling blood pressure and heart rate. We had only minutes left. Judging by our light headedness, consciousness would go sooner.

(Angel.)

(Sir?)

(I'm sorry, but I have to survive.)

His amusement rippled through us both. (It's not going to matter. Look.)

My attention shifted toward our dimming vision. Between traveling patches of dark-fluggy dizziness, we blinked clear. Angel turned his head to show me some figures lowgrav skipping toward the abutment.

They wore armored EVs, carried weapons and wore air tanks on their backs. Obviously not our guys. A Terran patrol.

Their scanning frequencies brushed around the Angel's open receiver. It gave me an idea. I rather have a whole, healthy body, even if it only breathed oxygen. And the intelligence would be priceless if I could get it back to our people. Well, once more into the breach. (Farewell, Angel)

(Sir. No!)

I jumped flesh again.

The grunt that I volted into never knew what hit him. Maybe my incoming was too much of a shock for him. He blew out like a candle. He did the Big Evac. Jumped into the Null Receiver. Anyway, it didn't make my landing any softer. It's not as easy as drone jumping. Their neurons are designed for generic refits. When the kid dropped his body, his body dropped, too. I went with it. The whole dusty, rocky, red world whirled away down the drain. For a second, I thought I had jumped into the Big Null, too.

When I came to, opening fresh eyes to the clean, white ceiling of a Terran MASH I was instantly aware of my breath. Did it feel warm and thin because it was O_2 and not the iron-talc laden CO_2 I was used to? I used to wonder if breathing O_2 felt any different than breathing CO_2. The whole O_2 thing always sounded backward to me until my induction briefing. Then I found out that we were the ones engineered with plant genes that gave us a respiratory system that processes CO_2. It made us cheap, easy labor for all the building and terraforming they planned. It sickens me to know that they use our very breath against us. We draw in the native air and expel unbound oxygen. Between our breath and their behemoth O2 generators, the changes - our leaders say - will be exponential. One day, the balance will tip. Everybody calculates a different Dooms O2 Day. One thing is for sure. They will rejoice; pull off their air tanks and shut down their O2 generators while we strangle and die on the rock strewn plains of our own world. Our purpose served, we'll be just corpses to gather and churn into compost.

Somewhere nearby, the thug-thug of chugging MASH O2 generators leaked through the walls of the recovery unit. It occurred to me that I wore a Terran body and it was entirely possible for me to suffocate on my own planet now.

Swimming through the razor burn of the last occupant's memories, my consciousness settled into its new residence. Some of the kid I just killed would always linger in the background, nagging my thoughts, mixing with them a little, but eventually the chemical signatures of his memories would disintegrate and would fade like old nightmares do, only popping up every now and again in reflex or maybe for the sake of penance. The flip side was that those residuals would help hide me from the enemy. The grunt's memories made good camouflage.

"Easy, Private," somebody said, touching my shoulder. I dropped my gaze from the ceiling and noticed the nurse at my cot side. He looked beside him. "Captain, he's awake."

I followed the nurse's gaze. The platoon commander was in the cot next to me. He sat up and looked me over with steel colored eyes. For an instant, I thought I saw something there. I thought I saw Angel. Well, it was wishful thinking. Waking up this deep behind enemy lines, it was only natural. Without a standard drone issue, I felt a little naked.

"Did we get those last two Cooties, Captain?" I had to play along. The kid's natural enthusiasm lingered among his synapses. Faking it was a little too easy.

He nodded. "We got 'em, Private." He glanced at the nurse which told me something was up. He told me, "You dropped for no reason, Private. You remember what happened?"

"Yes Sir. One of those Cooties tried to jump me through my com unit. I caught him coming in and cut my receivers."

"How much of him got in, Son?"

"I'm not sure. I stopped him, that's for certain … but," it was better not to tell too big a lie, "I feel a little off."

The nurse said, "His neural print was altered, Captain."

The Captain frowned and told me, "Sorry, Private, but you're out of the game until we're sure you weren't compromised."

"Yes, Sir."

"Lieutenant, put a guard on him. Once he's released, I want him quarantined for seventy-two hours. Take prints every four hours."

"Yes, Sir."

Buying a little trust, I nodded at the Captain's cot. "Sir?"

"Yes, Private."

"Sir, are you all right?"

He huffed. A sly smile slid across his leathery face. He glanced down at his legs.

I noticed the his right cuff was cut off and his leg was bandaged from knee to ankle.

The Terran Captain said, "The price of over confidence. I walked up to that Cootie wardog's hacked up drone with my pulser cocked up. Don't you know that bastard spun around on his belly and slashed open the leg of my suit with a bowie knife. Took out my left hamstring. Never expected one of those things to go low tech like that. I went down firing. Splattered what was left of that damned thing and blew it clean off the end of the abutment."

It was impossible not to show some rage, but I had to camouflage it somehow, so I said, "Son of a bitch." I meant it for the Terran Captain.

The Captain snorted a laugh and shook his head. "No bitch gave birth to that thing, Private."

"No, Captain. I suppose not." Before I leave, I'm going to slit that bastard's throat. Angel might have gone a little nuts at the end and tried to take me with him, but I don't blame him. He was dying and he was in pain. That does crazy shit to a man; drone or wardog. It doesn't matter. He didn't deserve to have his guts spattered all over the abutment. He deserved better.

When I was released from the infirmary, two MPs escorted me to an eight square pop-up and locked me in. I guess they figured three Terran days was all they needed to figure out whether I was a Terran or a Cootie. They could've kept me in that pop-up for three Terran years. It wouldn't have made a difference. My mnemes had completely integrated the kid's mnemes. The Terran quack could take all the scans he wanted. All the spikes and dips on their EEGs would match up line for line from now on.

At least I got an eye full on the way over. It stimulated the kid's memories. The Terrans had bubbled up a big base on the north ledge of the Vallis, probably just a few kilos from the aqueduct Angel and me just blew. Inside the geoplast, there were pop-ups for every thing from mess and storage to barracks and equipment. This was a monster of an operation. Those MPs walked me passed the housing for the shield generator, close enough for me to hear the turbines humming away in there. I realized that the webbing overhead wasn't ordinary support work for the bubble, but had to be one of those reflector nets that our Intelligence reported. It meant our air recons would never see this camp. As we turned down a path between rows of detention pop-ups, I caught a glimpse of the rocky fields that lay just beyond the bubble.

I saw silky black space wings with heavy laser mounts under their noses. Not a hundred, or even hundreds, but a thousand at least. Perfect rows of them that went on and on and on. Every one of them tarped with the same webbing that covered the bubble. The kid remembered that the Terrans were building toward a major offensive. The idea was to obliterate as many Cootie rebels as possible and break the back of the Resistance once and for all. That hit me like a punch. I might have been the only wardog who knew about it. My gut started a slow, sickening slide as we stepped to the door of the pop-up.

As the MPs opened my cell door, one of them grinned, "Home sweet home."

My muscles spasmed; a stalled reflex to turn and attack. I almost went for them right there, but it just wasn't the right moment. A better one would come. I couldn't escape yet. I needed to when the assault was. I stepped in. The door thunked shut behind me. I sat down on my cot, noticed evening rations on the little drop down shelf beside me and realized that three days might be too long to wait. Three days might be all the Terrans need to overrun our positions. We had been blowing up aqueducts and agrobubbles for two years. All the time gaining numbers, strength and organization; putting an ugly dent in the Terran claim to Mars. I suppose we poked the bastards a little too hard. But, the truth is we were going to have to poke them even harder before this was through. A lot harder.

Unfortunately, as much as I dredged my host's memories, the kid simply didn't know when the offensive was going to happen. He just filled me up with anxious anticipation. Or, maybe that was mine.

This master race from Earth uses us so carelessly, so selfishly. We were made to live on this world, walk these rocky plains, breathe this dusty, cold air. I noticed the kid's hands … my hands now. Young, uncalloused. A new recruit. A glad recruit. A stupid, young kid who gobbled down propaganda with his evening chow.

Well, my soul is still Martian. That's all that matters. For now I'm one of them; sitting in this bubble like a guppy in a fish bowl, gulping lung fulls of this rarefied, humid syrup they call air, feeling puny and cold. If I didn't hate Terrans so much, I might feel sorry for them. They're so desperate. They're so scared of this planet and how easy it can kill them. I think that's what makes them so scared of us. We're part of Mars. We are the boulder strewn deserts and that soft, hazy sky. We're it. We're the planet come to life to kick their pink O-2 sucking asses all the way back to Earth where they fuckin' belong.

I shook off the kid's blood lust as well as mine, then noticed supper again.

It was some kind of beans in a runny red sauce. My mouth watered, so it must have been something the kid liked. What the Hell, his 'buds are mine now. I picked up a fork and dug in. With Plan A whacked, I'll have to figure out a Plan B … after evening rations.

Long passed lights out, I watched the compound through the little, grilled window of my pop-up. Guards strolled across my line of view several times each hour, at random intervals and they were well aware that I was awake and watching them. Even though I stood back from the window, they glanced over at me as they passed. There must have been some kind of sensor in their headsets, or maybe on the pop-up itself. I could have just body vaulted again, but it was too risky here. They were watching me. As soon as the kid's body dropped dead, they would know a Cootie was in camp. I had to stay camouflaged little longer. Once I get back to my own company, they'll scan me, recognize my mnemonic pattern and refit me. It'll be good to breathe Martian air again. There's something nasty and whorish about breathing O-2. Until then, all I've got is this kid's body and the knowledge in his head. Hopefully, it'll be all I need.

I stepped close to the grill as the guard came by. My new brain knew him. "Hey, Billy."

He stopped and looked over. "Jon?"

"I think you better get the Captain."

"Why?" He kept his distance.

"The Cootie that jumped my com definitely left some of himself behind before we splattered him. I think it's intelligence data."

"From a drone, Jon?"

"Wasn't the drone that jumped me, Billy. It was the wardog. He jumped his own drone before he fell into the gorge."

"How come you didn't say anything about that before now?"

"Because it was all jumbled up in my head. I've been sorting it out. I think I better talk to the Captain, Billy. The Cooties know about the offensive."

He cursed softly, turned away and opened a com frequency. I knew because my receivers crackled faintly, although I couldn't pick up the transmission. Of course, he sent it on a secure channel.

My only worry was that the Captain would come to me, instead of having me brought to him. I hoped for the arrogance of rank would overwhelm prudent judgment. After a minute or so, two more MPs stepped up to Billy. These guys I only knew by sight. They glanced my way then they came toward my pop-up.

One looked in through the grill. "Stand back from the door, on the X. Face to the wall. Hands on your head. Fingers interlaced."

I assumed the position.

The door opened. I didn't have to see them to know that two pulser rifles were trained on my skull. The skin there instinctively cringed, making my hair stand up.

"Turn around and take eight steps out of the cell."

I obliged, stepping into chilly night air. Firearms tracked my progress. The sky was murky dark, not many stars and pressing toward dawn already. I didn't ask them where they were taking me. They wouldn't have answered. Beside, it was obvious. Sometimes, the only weapon a soldier needs is his enemy's arrogance.

Even without my old implants I could sense the thousands and thousands of bodies gathering under the enormous network of the bubble. The anticipation of carnage lingered like high humidity; damp and close to the skin. For a troubling moment, I couldn't distinguish it from fear, but then maybe that's all it was. Theirs and mine.

We left Billy behind at the detention area which was a small relief. My stolen memories would have plagued me with guilt if I killed one of the kid's favorite drinking buddies. As for the MPs .... I moved along quietly, noting the landmarks, having already picked the spot I would strike. In an unfamiliar body, I wasn't purely certain of its agility or reflexes, although the kid seemed fit enough. At least, he had been through reduced G boot camp. So, I waited until we turned down the walkway that ran behind the generator housing, where the shadows on the building were heaviest. Then, I ... sagged toward the wall, raising an arm to catch myself on the corrugated wall. I let out a little groan, already knowing that one of my escort would move in to assist me while the other held his weapon on me.

"Private."

I never liked using a man's compassion against him, but this is war, right? I straightened, pretending weak legs, "It's that Cootie, I think. I don't know." I gave my head a shake. "Feel strange." He gripped my elbow, I glimpsed his weapon sag, muzzle down, then I glanced at his partner. He saw me look at the weapon. He saw what was my eyes. He was smart, he just wasn't fast enough. Twisting back, I got an arm behind the MP who bent in help me. I shoved him toward the prongs of the taser just as it went off. He was hit and thrown back to me, his paralyzed gun arm flinging up. I grabbed at the trigger, squeezing off a charge, peppering the air with bolts. As much as I hated to bring the whole camp down on my neck with the crackle of more discharge, I wanted the other MP to stop shooting at me long enough for me to make a run for it. I needed those precious seconds out of his cross hairs.

It worked. He rolled. I ran, scooping up the convulsing soldier's weapon as I went. I ducked behind the generator then zagged into the maze of equipment pop-ups. I knew I could make it as far as the airlock on the north side of the bubble. I needed a suit, but I would worry about that when I got there. The kid's knowledge of the base helped.

Yet, I heard Terran soldiers rolling out of their barracks. I heard them swarming into the maze after me. The terror of that moment on the edge of the aqueduct hit me again. This was worse than staring down into that gorge. This was worse than certain death. When those bastards catch me …. Visions of the torture techniques that kid had learned flowed through me, paralyzing my psyche. It was almost like that kid was still alive inside my head, trying to terrorize me, to slow me down until the others could catch up to me. *Fuck*. I am going to die the worst way possible. I almost hared out. *Fuck*. Maybe Angel was right. War isn't worth this. Nothing is worth this. Legs aching-draining with fear, I dug deep, beneath all that. A monster named Survival pumped my legs. I let him take over. I went numb. I ran like Hell. I ran from Hell.

Skidding to a stop along the last wall of a big pop-up before the lock, I panted as silently as I could and pressed my weapon close to my chest. Heart hammering in my ears, I looked into smoky iris of the airlock not twenty meters from where I stood. It looked empty. According to my new brain, they weren't ordinarily guarded, but operated on a palm print locking system. With the panic, I didn't think anyone had thought to void my print, but they would any second. I looked up into the flood lights on the webbing of the bubble. There could have been snipers posted up there. I shook off my paranoia. They couldn't possibly have had time to climb up there. I gulped a breath, clearing my head a moment, then leaned out to look around the corner, praying there was no one in sight, praying there weren't snipers in the webbing even though I knew there couldn't be. Every thing looked clear-

Sudden pain creased the back of my neck; a blow like a thunderclap and the world spun. I barely felt the headlock, but I felt the body slam. My lungs collapsed instantly, I sprawled on my back in the dirt, dusty plumes gushing up around my body, wheezing and paralyzed as a big figure dropped on me and jammed something with a cold edge up under my throat. He didn't kill me right away. He let me catch my breath first.

It was the Terran captain. He held the Angel's old bowie knife to my throat.

"Shhhhh." He said, then glanced around us. I kept my eyes on him. My skin pimpled cold at the sound of Terran soldiers scuffling around only a few hundred yards away. The captain looked down at me at last. His pale eyes narrowed. I glanced toward the taser. I dropped it when he grabbed me. He noticed, huffed and kicked it away. Then he eased back, lowering the knife. He got up. I noticed he was wearing the bottom half of an EV suite. He offered me a hand.

I didn't take it, but I got to my feet, neck aching, chest hurting and ears listening to the voices of the Terran soldiers as they rustled through the pop-ups. They sounded as if they were moving away.

The captain told me, "I've commed them that this area is secure. They're moving down the perimeter to search for you." He pointed with Angel's knife toward the airlock. "I can get you to the gorge. After that, you're on your own."

I nodded at his leg; the one Angel cut "On that?"

"Got a STIM box on it. Don't feel a thing."

"You're helping me escape? Why?"

He blinked. Something familiar lit in his steel colored eyes. "Why do you think?"

Was I really seeing it? Was that Angel in his face? Did my drone really volt into the Terran captain? I didn't know and I wasn't going to stand there and play twenty questions with a entire company of angry Terran infantry looking for me.

"This way." He turned and limped toward the airlock. I followed him, thinking about the grin he wore when he described how he splattered my drone off the abutment.
I started to think about revenge.

We climbed into EV suits inside the lock, strapped on tanks, then left the bubble and headed out over the rocky fields. Once we were out of view of the bubble, the Terran captain pulled up and turned to me. Gaze burning too bright in the bowl of his helmet, he said, "You don't recognize me, do you?"

I eyed him.

"It's me. Your drone. Angel."

I squinted not quite believing him, though I wanted to. This could easily be some kind of trick.

"I volted into the Captain when I hamstrung him. When he went down, no one suspected a thing. My body had already gone over the abutment. He-I was bleeding all over the place. When he passed out from my incoming, his troops thought it was just from the pain."

I clung to doubt, but something familiar melted into his expression. Maybe.

He said, "I can prove it." The Terran smiled as he reached into the thigh pocket of his suit and pulled out a slip of paper. It tumbled open, unribboning all the way to the ground, stirring iron oxide dust devils. It was a brain scan. He held it out to me.

"They scanned you?"

"I scanned myself so I could prove what I'm saying. Look at it."

I dropped my eyes. I knew Angel's spikes and dips by heart. How many times had we jumped bodies? How many times did we sit in the buffer of some satellite, our mnemonic signatures idling in the hum of the maintenatrix until a rescue beam strobed in and pulled us out? Dozens? Hundreds?

That was Angel's scan on the scroll. A queer sort of weight sank through me. I guess it was relief. I wondered though, how much was really him. He wanted to die on the edge of that jagged aqueduct. He tried to take me with him. "You had a sudden change of heart."

"I suppose so." He chuckled. Very un-Angel like. Angel was a solemn sort of man … even stoic in a paternal sort of way. All drones are. They're programmed that way. I decided that part of him was still the Terran captain. It broke my heart a little. Even if I could have taken him with me when I escaped, he probably couldn't be salvaged. His mnemonic signature had been contaminated. Angel folded up the scan hard copy as he told me, "You know when I jumped, it really wasn't because I wanted to, Wardog. I wanted to die. But programming took over. I always thought that my obedience, my loyalty was a matter of duty, but it turned out to be a reflex. I couldn't fight the instinct to follow you, to continue with you. So here I am."

I watched him. "But you've changed."

He chuckled, nodding. "Integrating Captain Halsey altered my signature."

"Did he null, Angel?"

Angel eyed our dingy dawn. After too long a hesitation, he said, "I think so."

My spine crawled. This was worse than I thought. Angel wasn't sure. He was worse than contaminated. He had been corrupted.

"I still have his memories. I know everything he knew." Angel nodded in the direction of the bubble. "You saw the fleet?"

"The space wings? Yeah." I nodded slowly, swallowing, not sure how much I could trust him any more. Considering I used to trust him with my life, it was a scary, scary feeling.

"The Terrans aren't going to give up Mars, Wardog."

I squinted at him. "They aren't part of it. They don't belong to it like we do."

He chuckled, teeth flashing in the dark. "Have you looked at yourself lately? Neither do we any more. We're part of the ruling class now, or we can be. Don't you wonder what that'd be like?"

"I don't have to wonder. A few hours in this body is all I can stand of it already."

He eyed me as his smile faded. For a moment, the Terran captain looked out those gray eyes. His gaze thickened with hatred. His fist tightened on the hilt of the bowie. Then, the Terran captain was gone. Angel emerged again. He said, "You know I can't go back."

I nodded. "Of course." I was perfectly willing to let him stay here, to live out his life in the Terran captain's body. He had been a good drone. Trusting him less by the second, I eased passed him. "I better move along. They'll make a sweep this area eventually."

Eying me, Angel said, "They will."

"Good bye, Angel."

He nodded vaguely. Just as I started to turn away, he said, "It's interesting, isn't it?"

I faced him again. Several meters away, the distance reassured me. Shadow wrapped, his frame hulked in the mustard tinged sunrise. "What is?"

"Being Terran. Aside from what we breathe. We're not all that different. Not really." His smile lingered as he looked down at his boots. "I think I like it."

I laughed. "Well, you better. Because you're stuck with it."

I couldn't quite make out his expression behind the dust shield, but the intensity of his silence was plain enough. It gave me an ugly feeling, then he said, "So are you."

He raised the gun I had taken from the MP and shot me in the chest.

The force of the voltage knocked me back into a cluster of rocks. He started walking toward me, pulling the trigger again and again, frying me in that EV suit.

After, barely hanging onto consciousness, wadded in the smell my burned, dead flesh, the Angel leaned into my pain.

"Come ahead." He opened his com to me.

I sputtered, "No." I rather die right here in this kid's body first.

He knelt over me, picked up my head and said, "I'll help you."

My com receiver opened on its own. The son of a bitch tried to suck me clean out of that kid's head. Clinging to the transmitter, I heard myself gurgling, "No." I fought him, trying to slam off my receivers, but they wouldn't shut off. The taser charges wrecked them. As the whole world whirled away down the drain. So, I let go of my host body and went spinning away. If Angel-Halsey wants me, then he's going to get me.

And, I'm going to get him!

When I came to, I was lying in the rocks. Even through my EV filters, the smell of charred flesh lingered. I wasn't quite sure where I was until I sat up, smeared a layer of orange talc from my dust shield and saw the private's body laying a meter or so off to my right. The chest of his suit was thoroughly scorched and still smoking slightly. The ghostly tendrils curled and blew away on the rising dawn wind. I leaned over and wiped off his shield. Sleepy surprise slitted his dead eyes.

I got to my feet. There was no time to waste. I had to get moving. I had regrets, but they were well worth the price. It's a crime to waste such a good soldier and a good friend, but only one of us can command these synapses. I turned out to be stronger and the only one willing to make the sacrifice. There are so many lives at stake.

The Terrans were right. It's better to end this with just a few thousand deaths and let one flag be planted, then balance the terror and bring on the slaughter of millions for untold years to come. If there must be war, then let it be a swift excision with as little blood shed as possible. Mars is red enough.

I started the long walk back, leg aching while a littler war waged inside my head. Wardog fought me every step of the way back to the bubble, but I am his drone and I was made to protect him.

Always.

First published in *Aphelion Science Fiction Webzine*, July 1999.

THE DEATH CAT

The springs on the bottom of his chair whimpered as Administrator Robbins leaned back behind his desk. Gazing at Willie Kutbusch, he steepled his fingers over his vest as the corners of his mouth curled slowly into a patronizing smile. Like smoky thoughts escaping administrator's head, dust whirled in the light of the long window at his back. They stared at each other a long time, each quietly assessing the depth of madness in the other.

Ever since he was committed to Seneca Lake, Kutbusch maintained that he was not insane, but a victim of social ignorance. Naturally, the staff took his obstinacy as confirmation of the depth of his delusion. Yet, he possessed such a mild nature they responded in kind, gently insisting on his course of treatment. Having no other choice he complied. For the most part, the counselors found his condition little more than a mental aberration and a tedious, uninteresting one at that. To his relief, new attendings never paid him much attention. They were eager to rush onto the psychotics' ward like gleamy eyed, giggling children rushing to the lions' cage at the zoo.

They loved their mad lions.

When Kutbusch occasionally spent a day or two mired in a melancholy daze or skulked through the halls in mumbling agitation, it was only from the unrelenting aggravation of being locked up at the Lake; a sort of osmotic absorption of the great sea of madness that perpetually threatened to drown what was left of his sanity.

The chair yelped as the administrator sat forward, apparently ready to engage Kutbusch in their annual game. "What year did you arrive here, Willard?"

It was the year the Yankees beat Philadelphia, four to nothing. It was the year Nat King Cole sang, "*Mona Lisa ... Mona Lisa ....* ", Hoppy was big with the kids and Kutbusch never missed the *Hit Parade*. He just received his citizenship. The terrors of Bergen-Belsen almost left behind, he had just begun to relax and revel in the ideals of the American Dream. He practiced his English constantly until his pronunciation was nearly flawless. He began to consider his own dreams. That is until the night his land lady's calico cat brushed up against his leg in the dark hall outside his room. He panicked, thinking it was Katze.

Startled, he kicked out. The animal struck the wall with a crack then collapsed on the floor. Twisted and broken, it yowled once, voice ringing up through the halls, spiraling up the flights of stairs, to fall silent high in the darkness. Yet, the raking echo contorted Kutbusch's life like that dead cat on the floor.

He didn't mean to kill it. He never killed any thing before. Katze did that. That was what Katze was made to do.

His land lady called the police. After that night, they came to his door any time something bad happened in the neighborhood. *Like the Nazis*, he thought when he was most frightened. He tried to tell them that he thought it was Katze pressing up against his pant leg in the hall that night. They just stared. He tried to tell them that it was Katze in Bergen-Belsen. He tried to tell them. All through history. It was Katze. Katze. Katze. Katze. He knew from the look in their eyes that he should have never said a thing. Even using perfectly inflected English, he couldn't make them understand. Americans knew nothing of the old country stories. Ancient truths still live in the forests and lakes and hillsides of Europe. In a young country so full of new dreams, there was no room for old nightmares.

That's when the men from the hospital came.

Kutbusch noticed the administrator still waiting for his answer. "I came here in 1950, Mr. Robbins."

Robbins smiled wider and nodded, rocking a little in his chair, making it shriek softly over and over.

He tisked, "Ten years. You've been here ten years, Willard."

"Yes, Sir. That is why I believe it is time for me to be released."

The administrator frowned. "How so?"

"There is so little bed space, Sir. I myself have not so serious a malady as some."

"So it's out of generosity that you wish to be released."

Kutbusch dropped his eyes, feeling heat rise in his cheeks. He wasn't very good at lying. Couching his intention in some half-baked attempt at altruism seemed just as deceptive. The truth was he just wanted to be let out. "I feel that I am not so ill as to need the services of an institution, Mr. Robbins. I'm not a danger to any one. I can take employment. I'm a steady worker. I've proven that."

Robbins lifted the letter of recommendation briefly from his desk. "Chaplain Gray thinks very highly of you, Willard." His frown stretched. "But the good chaplain is not a psychiatrist. He ministers to the spirit. We minister to the mind."

"Does not one direct the other?"

The administrator raised a brow, making a mental check mark of the comment. It was a sure sign that he took Kutbusch's remark as a challenge and only incorrigible patients challenged the staff.

Incorrigible patients were not released. His chance at freedom slipped silently away again.

"Do you have family who can take care of you, Willard?"

Kutbusch eyed him. The administrator knew he didn't. He had only been in America a few years before he was taken to the hospital. He lost his parents and his sister in Bergen-Belsen. He would have died there too, if not for the British. His first memory of freedom was the salty scent of the English soldier who carried him out of the barracks and the chocolate bar he gave Kutbusch. "American," the soldier told him in German. It was so sweet, it made his jaws cramp; liberty in brown and silver foil.

Swallowing a fresh wash of saliva for the phantom flavor of freedom, Kutbusch told Robbins, "no, Sir."

"Then there wouldn't be any sense in you leaving then. You need support, Willard." Robbins sat back smiling. "We're here to support you."

Kutbusch sighed softly. He thought of his work for the chaplain. "Then may I be paid for digging?"

"Paid? What do you need money for, Willard? We buy you clothes and shoes. You have food to eat. Books to read." He laughed, "you cost us a fortune in chocolate bars. Do you know that? What in God's name do you need money for?"

Escape, Kutbusch thought. It seemed the only way he was going to leave the Lake. If he saved enough from digging for bus fare, he might slip under the fence after 'lights out' and run into town. He could buy a bus ticket and easily disappear any where in America. It was a big country. There was always work for a man with a strong back. If he could dig in the chaplain's cemetery, he could dig anywhere. He was still young. He could take a wife, settle down and remember how it is to be normal again. He would never talk about Katze again. Ever.

"I'll tell you what, Willard. Look me in the eyes and tell me that you don't believe in your gift any more. If you can do that, I'll sign your release papers myself."

Of course, Kutbusch couldn't do that, so he looked at his mud crusted work boots.

"You see, Willard. You're not ready."

"May I ask you something, Mr. Robbins?"

The administrator raised his brows.

"It's about my gift."

"Yes?"

"Have you ever known me to be wrong?"

The administrator's expression fell still. Even his ever sinking-rising brow ceased twitching and hung in a rare moment of suspended opinion. He couldn't deny it, but neither could he admit that, yes, Willard had never been wrong. Of course, a simple reply to the affirmative would have meant more than a shattering of the administrator's dominance over his charge, or that Kutbusch had been wrongly institutionalized for the past decade, or that Kutbusch was right and the administrator was wrong. It meant that reality was not how the administrator thought it should be. His orderly, numbered and slotted world was not orderly, numbered and slotted. Some of those whose behavior could be assigned a category of mental illness were not necessarily sick, but might be enlightened beings shackled by the social prejudices of the ignorant. That would mean that the administrator was one of the later and he prided himself on being of the former. So the columns of framed degrees hung on the wall beside him indicated. It meant that scholars of the psyche were no more adept than a simple Austrian borne grave digger when it came to matters of the spirit and the ways in which death might choose to visit any one of them.

"You know, Willard, the human mind has a penchant for making connections and finding patterns. Sometimes that mechanism makes a faulty connection between two disparate events. Do you understand what I'm saying?"

"Yes." Kutbusch answered, but he was well aware that he was not the one who habitually patched his fraying gestalt with thread bare psychiatric platitudes. Looking out the tall office window, Kutbusch noticed several patients out on the east lawn playing crocket. He saw Katze out there with them. It swarmed over a young woman, clung to her shoulders and licked delicately at her brow. His conscience panged faintly. He nodded. "Another one is going to pass soon."

Robbins squinted. "Who then?"

It made Kutbusch a little sad to admit, but he said, "Sara Bennett."

"Don't be ridiculous, Willard. Sara just came to us. She's schizophrenic, but physically she's young, strong and in perfect health."

Kutbusch shrugged. "She has the look."

"And what look is that, Willard? You always talk about `the look' of them before they die, but you've never described it. Can you describe it?"

Kutbusch eyed him, studying the places Katze was most likely to cuddle up on the administrator. It seemed to nestle in strange places; the crook of the neck, the hollows of the eyes, along the slack flesh of the jowls or the plains of the cheeks. In those places it settled and began to lick away at life contently. Inside and out, the human body was a great landscape of opportunities to it. It slinked around everyone's form sooner or later, rough tongue lapping casually here, then there. Sometimes it licked for only a few days, or weeks, but most often for years. Katze was a patient hunter when it came to souls.

"Willard, why are you looking at me like that?"

For a moment, Kutbusch wickedly wished he saw Katze on the administrator, but he wished for it a hundred times before over the years and nothing ever happened. One thing Kutbusch was sure of, for all the times he saw Katze coming he could not will it to service, but merely witness its habit as it stalked its next victim, then wiggled gently beneath their hair, their clothes and skin, gradually licking loose the ties of life that fastened the spirit to the body. He seemed to see most clearly the decay of those bonds to life as they dwindled, fraying as that invisible tongue chafed them over and over, hour after hour, day after day, patiently, persistently until the threads finally gave away and the spirit floated loose.

How could he describe that to the administrator? Robbins was no a man of metaphysical notions, but of physiology and chemistry; a creature of such taunt intellectual sinew that no meaningful soul could rest comfortably in his marrow. In so many ways, he was like Katze itself; driving the tongue of psychological doctrine over his charges for hour upon hour, day upon day, winnowing away the ties of sanity until their minds floated loose at last. Perhaps, he was worse than Katze. It had no passion for its work. Like wind and water it was simply one of the forces of nature, but the administrator loved the taste of decaying sanity. He craved it and thrived on it. It gave him purpose and power.

If Kutbusch could have wished death on anyone, he would have wished it on Robbins.

"Did you hear me, Willard? Describe this look of death you see."

Kutbusch frowned and looked out the window, ignoring the administrator's agitation. "I only know the look when I see it. I can't describe it."

"That's the convenience of a delusion, isn't it, Willard? If only you can experience it, then no one else can disprove it. You keep control that way, Willard. You need control, don't you?"

"In a place like this, Mr. Robbins, who does not?"

The administrator's eyes glittered a moment then quieted. There was nothing he resented more than a patient who challenged his management of the institution. Yet, to Kutbusch every question the administrator put to him seemed one he should try answering for himself. He seemed to be the most delusional individual in the place. Weary of the game, he told Robbins, "I have my own counselor."

"And I think I'll have a talk with Doctor Meager. He needs to schedule more sessions with you. You're back sliding, Willard."

"How so, Mr. Robbins?"

"Well, your behavior here for one thing. You're becoming obstinate and contrary. I can't have that. Patients must maintain an ordered and disciplined discourse with the staff, or else we would have anarchy."

"Whether you like it or not, Mr. Robbins, life," Kutbusch told him quietly, "is anarchy." Perhaps so many years of quiet frustration got the better of him, but he leaned forward in his seat and insisted, "Young Sara Bennett has the look. And. I am not mad. I never was."

"Silence!" The administrator rapped the desk with his open hand. "That is insubordinate, Willard. Orderly!"

The big, burly boy who escorted Kutbusch to his appointment stepped into the threshold, "yes, Sir."

"Escort Willard to his room for a twenty-four hour lock down. Inform Doctor Meager that his patient is acting out."

The big boy, Joe was his name, flicked his gaze at Kutbusch and lifted a hammy, young hand, "Come on, Willie."

Kutbusch obeyed. Resisting would only escalate the matter. He had seen plenty of patients erupt out of frustration only to be driven to the floor by a squad of orderlies, then bound or jacketed or sedated into submission. There was more dignity and less chance of injury by just going along.

As they stepped out the door, Young Joe said, "You shouldn't goad him like that, Willie."

"I only told him the truth."

Young Joe shrugged his brows and huffed. "Come on."

They started down the hall as the administrator thrust his head around the jamb. "And Joseph. He requires a jacket."

Young Joe actually stopped and faced Robbins. "Sir?"

"You heard me. A jacket."

Young Joe met Kutbusch's gaze. He frowned his regret.

"It's not your fault, Joe." Kutbusch told him softly.

"What did you say, Willard?" the administrator squinted.

"Nothing, Mr. Robbins."

"The jacket, Joseph."

"Yes, Sir."

That was how the administrator maintained order in his world and every one else's world as well.

One day of confinement stretched into two. Kutbusch spent most of it sitting on the edge of his bed, bound up in the jacket, gazing out the window of his room, grateful for a view of his sanity. He could watch the forested hillsides for hours, meditating on the distant autumn trees. With their leaves down, they gave the hillside a fine, gray, velvety texture. Once in a while he saw deer or a fox, sometimes a gaggle of wild turkeys cropping grass at the edge of the lawn just outside the fence.

At last, near supper time a key scraped in the lock and the door swung open. Young Joe, Doctor Meager and Chaplain Gray stood there. The chaplain smiled gently. He held a tray full of covered dishes in his hands. "Good news, Willie. Jonathan made apple kuchen for desert tonight."

It was Kutbusch's favorite. Jonathan, the cook at the Lake, was a kind fellow who frequently baked for the solace of the patients. He did more good with a single pie or a batch of cookies than some counselors could do in a year of sessions. The chaplain stepped in ahead of the others, brought the tray and set it on the little table by the window.

Young Joe caught Doctor Meager's nod. He came to the bedside in a hurry to unbuckle the arms and back of Kutbusch's jacket. Muscles numb and limp from having been bent around his chest for so long, he had some trouble slipping his arms out of the sleeves. Meager stepped up and began rubbing the life back into them. Kutbusch couldn't help wincing a little. As the blood flow returned he suffered brutal pins-and-needles in his hands and fingers. Meager rubbed more furiously, growling, "there you are. Better?"

"Yes. Thank you."

No one made any apologies, but the scent of guilt lingered in the air.

"I spoke to Robbins, Willie, and we'll schedule a second session on Wednesdays," Doctor Meager said, grave gray eyes flicking reluctantly up from his work massaging the tingles out of Kutbusch's hands. "They won't be long ones. Just a follow up to our usual Monday afternoon chats. All right?"

Kutbusch shrugged in agreement. Meager was bound to agree with the administrator's assessment. While he was generally a man of some conscience, he hadn't much courage so his moral cowardice and his conscience went to battle quietly in his stomach over the years. He had the ulcers to prove it. Katze got at Doctor Meager by licking away his moral fiber a strand at a time. Though he often tried to salve his conscience with compromise, the stuff only made the threads dissolve faster.

The chaplain ushered him to his meal, lifted off the covers and urged him to sit. He even popped the spout on the milk carton and filled the glass, then glanced at the others as he sat across from Kutbusch. "Willie, do you think you'll be all right to dig in the morning?"

Kutbusch raised his eyes from the steaming pork chop, mashed potatoes and green beans on his plate. He swallowed a tiny regret. "How did she die?"

"An aneurysm," Doctor Meager said, gesturing to his temple.

Kutbusch sighed quietly and looked over his food. He saw so many pass over the years that he found it no longer affected his appetite the way it used to. "She had no family to come claim her?"

"Sadly. No."

He nodded. Like so many others branded mad, pretty young Sara had been abandoned at the Lake, too. He picked up his fork and knife. "First thing in the morning, Chaplain?"

"Thank you, Willie."

They lingered, watching him. Kutbusch was aware that over the years he gained a reputation for knowing when others were about to pass. Although his gift was regarded outwardly as a manifestation of his delusional condition more than a few of the patients and staff a like privately reckoned his claim. Yet, no matter the mounting evidence of support for it over the years, they could never admit that they believed him. Look what happened to him when he revealed his gift and what is more, when he persisted in its existence. He noticed that whenever one of his predictions came to pass, their curiosity in him rekindled. More than that, they grew kinder for a little while as if being charitable to Kutbusch would shield them from Katze's tongue. He gradually grew accustomed to the tidal flow of their charity and learned to accept it with grace. He became as the angel, gently heralding the darkness. It was a curious kind of celebrity in this mad place.

Young Joe seemed to sense they lingered for no particular reason and said, "Do you need anything else, Willie?"

"No. Thank you."

The three shuffled out, leaving him alone with his supper. Yet, when the door closed Kutbusch found he hadn't the stomach for pork and potatoes after all. It was all ready so full of sadness, it ached. So he took his desert to the window, ate kuchen in the dark and watched the moon come up.

Though the morning started out with frothy gray skies and the lawns covered with frost, a warm sun soon burned through to melt it all away. With a good, square eight foot long by four feet deep wedge dug, Sarah's grave on the west edge of the cemetery was starting to take a fine shape by noon, so Kutbusch heaved the last spade of dirt onto the bed behind the little tractor and paused, hanging his hands on the point of his shovel handle while he caught his breath and looked across the cemetery.

Orderly and peaceful, white granite markers gazed back at him. Except for the fact that he didn't belong in an institution, he favored his work here. He liked the feel of his muscles straining and working. He liked to be in the elements, under sun or rain didn't matter much to him. He had even dug in the snow with relish. Pale flakes floated down to tickle his ears in mid December. It really wasn't until mid January that the ground froze and there was no grave making until the muddy month of April. Digging in April Kutbusch could do with out. The first few feet beneath the turf were always sloppy and heavy. Given that one reservation, digging was serene and steady. It was the solitary kind of work that complimented his disposition. The chaplain never bothered him except on the occasion of a hot day, when he would kindly bring a pitcher of water, or call Kutbusch in, insisting it was too hot for heavy work.

Kutbusch smiled a little at the hills beyond the fence line. Pretty soon they would be snow dappled and sleepy. He admired the quiet dependability of the seasons.

"Willard! There you are!"

Kutbusch closed his eyes, letting fresh tension release slowly from the muscles in his shoulders. By the time Administrator Robbins's grass muffled steps fell upon Kutbusch's ears, he was calm and resigned to the gloating approach of his lord and master on this earthly plain.

"Gray said that I'd find you here."

"Yes, Sir."

He stepped to the edge of the turf and raised his nose, glancing back and forth at the length and depth of the wedge. "For Sara?"

"Yes, Sir."

The administrator avoided Kutbusch's gaze, "First rate job as always, Willard."

"Thank you, Sir."

The administrator paused a moment, his brows alternately sinking and rising, like fuzzy puppeteers working the strings of his thoughts. At last, he said, "you know that it was a coincidence, Willard."

Kutbusch resisted an honest remark, but substituted by gently sloughing a few inches off a bit rough edge of wall on Sara's grave with his shovel.

"Don't you agree, Willard?"

"If you insist, Mr. Robbins." He didn't look up, but sloughed off another spade full, scooped and tossed it onto the bed. He began to dig again, reluctant to catch the administrator's eye, already knowing that his reply was not conciliatory enough. It leaked dissent. The only course was to resist engaging him in conversation and avoid another chance escalation that would only land Kutbusch again in isolation and possibly the jacket as well.

The administrator mumbled something then fell quiet as Kutbusch slipped into a comfortable digging rhythm. When he chanced a glance up from his spadework, the administrator studied the knoll along the edge of the cemetery. He said, "Willard, this is a very peaceful place."

"Yes, Sir."

"Did you know that I planted that chestnut tree there on the hill when I first arrived here. It's a good size now."

Kutbusch noticed it. "Handsome specimen. Fine spot to rest a while. Shady, Sir."

"It is, isn't it? I always thought it was a lovely spot, Willard. You know, I think I'd like to be buried there one day."

Kutbusch looked at him, fiendishly seeking signs of death's lick. Like always there wasn't anything particularly wearing on the bonds that tied the administrator's soul to his form. Kutbusch was disappointed.

It was unfair that someone so apt to whittle away at the minds and hearts of others went so wholly uncompromised for his crimes. And yet, maybe it was not so. "Won't you be buried with your family, Sir?"

"I have none, Willard."

Kutbusch blinked, "No parents?"

"We were estranged when I was young."

"No wife?"

"None, Willard, who would have me." The administrator scarcely admitted to the littlest smile; a flinch of long buried pain.

In that flicker of facial muscle, Willard spotted the first lazy lick. At the same moment he suffered a pang of sympathy. The administrator had caged himself up along with his inmates. Who knew why. No wonder he was a pitiless, controlling man. Kutbusch almost felt sorry for him.

"Why are you looking at me like that, Willard?" That quick, cooling squint reminded Kutbusch to take care. There was no use in admitting a moment of empathy. The administrator was too defensive for it. Without another word, Kutbusch bent into his digging again and continued until he heard Robbins say, "yes, I should like to be buried up there above all of you under that glorious chestnut tree. That way I can look down on you and shepherd you through all of eternity."

Kutbusch kept digging until he heard the administrator's shoes shuffle away over the crisp autumn rye. The idea of enduring Robbins's unwavering stare forever did not seem the kind of afterlife the patients at the Lake might hope for. Certainly, the thought made Kutbusch cringe.

Sitting quietly, his thick, callused old hands in his lap, Kutbusch watched a fly crawl up the calendar on the wall outside the administrator's office. It seemed to be making a deliberate effort to reach for the '1' in November, as if it thought it could go back in time merely by navigating the page. If it was that simple turn back time, Kutbusch would have crossed a continent of calendars and walked himself all the way back to that night, thirty years ago, when he kicked that damned cat.

Hot air blew out the register beneath his bench. The new furnace was much quieter than the old boiler, but Kutbusch missed the boiler a little. It belched and groaned through thirty winters like some tired, bored old beast in the basement.

That wasn't the only change in the place. Down the hall, young men in coveralls rolled fresh white paint over the gray walls. That alone seemed to bring new light into the halls and new life to the patients. The lighting and wiring had been updated. The leaks in the chapel roof were fixed. Kutbusch puzzled that so many changes had been made so quickly. He wished Meager could have been there to see it, but he passed away last year exactly one year to the day after his retirement party. Stomach cancer got him.

Just then Chaplain Gray stepped out of the administrator's office. He smiled and winked. "The old place is looking good, isn't it, Willie?"

"It is, Chaplain. What's going on?"

The chaplain bent close and whispered, "Health Department came through a few months ago. They didn't like what they saw. All this-" he waved his soft, wrinkled hand around, "-is just the tip of the iceberg. They're especially interested in revisiting patient care."

Kutbusch nodded slowly. He noticed the administrator's attitude seemed more dyspeptic than usual in recent months. No doubt, Robbins did not care for the state meddling in the way he ran his mad house. If he was in one of his moods, he would surely deny Kutbusch's appeal for release again.

This year, he hoped that with affidavits from his new counselor, some of the staff and the chaplain, he stood a better chance. He had stopped predicting deaths. Submitting himself to a show of the kind of sanity that the administrator demanded. Kutbusch was worn down. He had grown tired of facing release denials every year. Worse than that, he felt himself growing comfortable at the Lake, relinquishing the dream of freedom a little bit more each November. He almost didn't care if he ever left. That is until Meager died with a belly full of tumors. The compromise of courage killed him, but Kutbusch realized that it might be just the thing he needed to set himself free. So, when he saw the Katze licking away at someone, he kept his mouth shut and looked the other way. He practiced not seeing it. He pretended Katze didn't exist.

Then the chaplain leaned toward him again and winked. "Things are looking promising, Willie."

A tiny thrill stumbled hesitantly through Kutbusch's chest. He wanted to hope for the best, but after so many years, and knowing the administrator as he did, doubt sat down with a sullen thud in his head. Yet, as he looked around him, the pretty white walls and fresh, glossy floors inspired him. Robbins couldn't refuse the state. At last, someone compelled him to humanity and common sense. Maybe the chaplain was right. Maybe Kutbusch would be released at last.

Gray must have caught the flicker of hope in his face. He smiled and patted Kutbusch's shoulder. "Go on in, Willie. And good luck."

Belly fluttering, Kutbusch stepped into the administrator's office. He stood with his back to Kutbusch, hands gathered behind him and looked out the window. White flakes flowed passed his window, thick and hypnotic.

"The first snow of the season, Willard."

"Yes, Sir."

"It'll melt off though. It's too early in the season to stick."

"Yes, Sir."

His form, grown narrow and rigid with age, turned from the pale veil of falling snow passed the tall window. In the dusky frame of his silhouette, Kutbusch thought he spotted something out of the ordinary.

Robbins came to his chair and sat. It groaned softly as he leaned back. His ever active brows, gray flecked, worked more slowly than usual. He stared at the open file on his desk too long. He seemed to slip into a light daze.

" Sir? Are you all right?"

"Of course," the administrator said as the slack flesh in his face tightened with the habit of renewed, if weary scrutiny.

"How long have you been here, Willard?"

Far too long, Kutbusch thought, but he said, "Thirty years, Sir."

He shuffled the papers in the open file almost hesitantly. There was a faint tremor in his fingertips; flesh jostled by that invisible, but unmistakable tongue. "Doctor Trieble feels you've made considerable progress in the past year."

"Yes, Sir."

"Do you feel you've made considerable progress, Willard?"

"I like to think so, Sir."

Robbins gazed at him a long while, brows rising and sinking, slowly, alternately like two tables of a balance scale gradually finding equilibrium. "Willard." He looked into Kutbusch's eyes purposefully. "Do you still believe you can see Death coming?"

Having a year of practice at shielding the look of knowing from his eyes, Kutbusch looked right into Robbins's eyes, passed the gentle, slow slurping at his brow, where it had already licked most of the hair from the top of his head and had set to work removing the color in his spindly side burns. "No, Sir. I cannot see Death coming."

Robbins stared at him a moment longer. "I see." He sat back, making his chair shriek softly. He shifted the papers and closed the file on his desk. "I'm sorry, Willard."

For a moment, Kutbusch was not sure what the administrator meant. He was so hopeful of the prospect of release for the first time in many years that he couldn't reckon any other answer. He sat there staring. " Sir?"

"I'm sorry, Willard," he repeated. "Maybe next year. You may go."

"Yes, Sir." He rose, legs a little weak with the queer notion that compromise had done him no more good than it did Meager in the end.

Desperate for some kind of solace, he turned and looked at Administrator Robbins to be sure that he saw what he saw.

What he could not do to win his own freedom in thirty years, it seemed time and Katze obliged. Meeting Robbins's eyes once more and for the last time, he said, "Goodbye, Sir."

Robbins squinted, mouth moving slightly as if to practice the shout for an orderly and probably the jacket, but he didn't shout at all. Bewilderment muffled his voice. Kutbusch walked out as that angry and uncertain stare borrowed into his shoulder.

The first few feet of the wedge came out quickly. Once his shock wore off, anger set in. The energy of it fueled Kutbusch's old muscles through good third of the grave. About the time that his outrage began to burn out, he noticed Chaplain Gray hurrying through the cemetery toward him, cassock snapping across his legs and they scissored along. "Willie. Willie."

He stopped digging. "Yes, Chaplain."

Breathless, Gray came to the graveside. "What are you doing?"

Kutbusch looked around him. Wasn't it obvious?

"You haven't said a word. Who's it to be this time?" The Chaplain looked over the grave. He jolted, "God in Heaven. It's not for you is it, Willie?"

"No, Chaplain, it's not for me." Resting a moment in his digging, Kutbusch hung his hands on the point of the spade handle and looked far across the lawn full of headstones up the hill at that glorious old Chestnut tree.

It stood; majestic trunk planted atop the wind billowed emerald swells of snow patched rye grass. Robbins was right. It was a lovely spot, shady, high and green. It was the perfect Eden to spend all of eternity.

Kutbusch told Gray, "When Katze gives me the nod, Chaplain, you'll know."

"How so, Willie?"

"I'll start turning up the sod under that old Chestnut tree."

First published in *The Quiet Ward Anthology*,
Prime Books, August 2003.

THYLACINE DREAMS

Goonda hunkered in the mud. He spread four dark fingers in a track then smiled wide. It was only a few hours old at most. This would please Eleanor. He looked over his shoulder and shouted, "here!"

She came quickly up the slope, lean legs scissoring through the bush. "You found something?"

"Waldagi track." He puffed through his wide, brown nostrils to blow off a fly crawling along his upper lip.

"Are you sure?"

"Look for yourself." He stepped back to let her see.

Eleanor squatted, looking track over then noticed the others around it. Blue eyes opening wider, she gasped, "there's must be six or seven different sets here."

Goonda's smile split, revealing perfect white teeth. Eleanor had good eyes for a white woman. She could read game track almost as good as a clansman. "I read seven. A family group. A pack, Eleanor."

She called over her shoulder, "Howard, thylacine tracks." She slipped a digital camera from a pocket of her flack jacket and began snapping pictures.

Goonda looked down trail. Howard Mullins labored up through knee high tussock. Loaded down with a top heavy back pack, he was red faced, puffing and in no hurry.

The clansman turned his back on the Australian. Mullins was one of those whites who still harbored subtle prejudice toward the clans. Since they started the climb, the scientist from Hobart was cool and dismissive. Goonda had a feeling that the Aussie was put off because he didn't offer to carry Mullins's load like a good abo should. Well, he wasn't a good abo. He was a tracker and a dreaming guide. Goonda had no doubt Sun Mother intended Mullins to bush walk to humility. He was happy to oblige Her.

As for Eleanor; he never met an American before, let alone one who was a scientist and a woman. Most of the people who paid him to take them through the bush were eco-tourists. They came in with gleaming, chrome framed back packs bulging with tents, air mattresses, ridiculous amounts of water and stacks and stacks of foil wrapped, dehydrated meals that they bought in Hobart. They came with expensive cameras then took endless pictures of koalas, sunsets, their authentic aborigine guide and each other. Jocular and arrogant, they trod heavily through the bush, scattering game ahead of them in all directions. They splashed naked around in the billabongs, hooted and hollered, playing at their idea of returning to nature; gleefully abandoning their dignity in the sacred rain forests on the steep, moist slopes of Federation Peak.

Sometimes, they would ask about the waldagi, calling it by its white name; the Tasmanian Tiger, but Goonda would tell them that it was gone, hunted to dust almost a hundred years ago.

"What about the reports … the sightings?" they would ask.

"Hoaxes," Goonda always told them. Lying was the only way to keep what was left safe from them. He noticed that even when they meant well, whites still tended to kill things.

Deep down, Goonda pitied them. Their spirits were hopelessly buried in the debris of their culture. All they knew were the glittery lies of television and the Internet. Yet, he kept leading bush walks through South West Park. He told himself he did it so that he could teach them about the Dreaming, to awaken their spirits, but after a few years leading the walks, he realized that most whites didn't understand. He started to believe they couldn't understand.

Then he met Eleanor.

With Mullins in tow, she arrived at Geevesville in one of Hobart Zoo's jeeps, without air mattresses, or plastic drums of water or foils of food. They left the jeep at the end of the park road, four days trek down the slope. All she took with her was a small backpack, a handful of electronics and curiously formidable blue eyes. Those eyes and her long, silky black braid of hair beguiled Goonda.

He watched her on the walk up. Unlike Mullins, unlike most whites, she moved through the bush almost soundlessly, quietly watchful, ears pricked to the voices of the highland rain forest. She had the sense of a clanswoman. She was a creature of the Dreaming like him, like his people. Goonda fancied Eleanor had been an aborigine once in a time before her white birth.

Impressed, he took her up the slope, away from the usual path along the coast, into the deep bush to show her the waldagi because he knew that when she saw it, she would realize that she could never tell the white world about it. Though she was a scientist, her eyes sparkled when she talked about the waldagi. She loved it like the Aborigine did. She would realize that the whites would only try to kill it again.

She would leave the waldagi alone.

Mullins was another matter. Goonda wanted to keep him as far from the den site as possible. He checked his collecting sack. Bush tomatoes half filled it. He had been plucking them off the side of trail as they went. The red ones were safe to eat. The green ones weren't. The Aussie would get the green ones for supper.

Water roiling in the pot over the sterno, Goonda eyed the flap to the tent to make sure Mullins and Eleanor weren't where they could see what he was doing as he cleaved wombat meat and tomatoes for stew. Storm clouds had moved in, but a tin collar kept the rain off the fire when it started. Heavy, cold tears from the sky began to pat-pat on Goonda's arms and shoulders while he cooked and plotted. Cold drops hissed and spat off the hot collar like the wise whispers of ancestors. Thick wisps of white smoke began to curl up from the sterno. Goonda made out forms and faces.

It was vision smoke.

Sun Mother wanted him to see something there. There were waldagi in the smoke. There were guns, too. Guns! Goonda leaned closer. Wisps of betrayal gusted through the vision. He drifted into a fire dreaming.

Rain pattering on the tarp overhead, Eleanor jacked the camera into her laptop then pulled up the pictures she took that morning. She didn't want to keep the computer on too long or else the battery would run down, but she wanted to make sure that she got some decent pictures. The only other photographs of thylacine tracks she knew of were the ones taken by Guiler in the sixties. They were intriguing, but not conclusive. She keyed the photos up.

Crisp. Clear. Perfect.

Cautious excitement tickled Eleanor's gut. Granted these weren't much more conclusive than Guiler's pictures, but they were only the beginning. She thought, Von Beringe felt this way when he saw the first mountain gorilla tracks. Like him, she built an evidence file. Like him, she would bring back a specimen. Only she didn't need an entourage of bearers and crates. All she need was her dart gun, the satellite phone and the chopper standing by down in Geevesville.

Howard leaned too close over her shoulder. Eleanor shrugged off a flash of annoyance. The Aussie had a knack for invading her space. She didn't particularly want him on the expedition, but it was funded by the zoo's money and they wanted a Hobart representative on the trip, so she didn't have a choice. "That bugger really works." He meant the digital camera. He reminded her, "but a few snaps of tracks won't be enough."

Eleanor glanced at the castings she made before the rain started. They dried on the tarped floor of the lean-to.

Howard caught her look and shrugged, "no more valid than those track castings of Bigfoot in the States."

Eleanor gritted her teeth. Howard had his own agenda. On the long drive to Geevesville all he talked about was the advances they made so far replicating thylacine genes. He was hooked on the idea of cloning a new pack of thylas from the last pup preserved in alcohol left in the Hobart

Museum specimen room. He wanted to use kangaroo eggs and a surrogate kangaroo mother. The more time Eleanor spent with Howard, the more she suspected he expected the expedition would fail. Even she knew it was more likely to fail than succeed. Her only hope was that their aborigine guide could find the animals. Goonda claimed to have seen them before high on the mountainside. More than that, Eleanor trusted him. The way he talked about them, she was sure he had seen thylacines on Federation Peak.

Yet, a few blurry photographs from 1962 and some anecdotal reports hardly proved that the species wasn't completely extinct. A live female would have made a better mother for a pup, cloned or not, than some damned kangaroo. Thylacines were predators not grazers. They wouldn't learn anything about thyla' behavior from a pup reared by a 'roo.

The first step was locating a pack and plotting their territory.

Listening to the rain beating steadily on the tarp, Eleanor wondered whether they would get that far. The fresh tracks Goonda found that morning melted away. By tomorrow, all the signs of the pack would be washed way. Even her tracker might not be able find them again.

Eleanor turned on her camp stool to prod at one of the drying plaster casts with her boot toe. She felt a stare and looked up. Howard eyed her.

"Do you have something to say?"

He shrugged his brows. "You really think we're going to find something up here, don't you?"

Eleanor huffed. There were moments that Howard was too much like her father. She spent her childhood growing up in tents on every plain, veldt, and rain forest between the Americas and Asia. He shot film for National Geographic. Howard was just as old school as her father. They were painfully pragmatic men. Trying to track and capture a live thylacine was preposterous to him. It was like chasing Bigfoot or believing in UFOs. "You really think trying to clone a sixty year old specimen is the only solution?"

"It's more of a sure thing that spending weeks in the bush chasing ghosts."

"Ghosts don't leave foot prints."

"Those could be wombat tracks."

"You know better than that, Howard. Look at the heel and toe placement."

Howard cocked his head at the castings. After a moment, he frowned.

"If you have don't believe in the expedition, why did you come?"

He smiled. "Ellie, are you that naïve? This is a publicity stunt. We're not going to find anything out here. We're not supposed to find anything out here." Howard pointed toward the drizzle beyond the tent flap. "That abo is just going to take us on a walk about through the park then we'll go home with some castings and more bloody useless pictures that zoologists can argue over for another decade." He shrugged. "But. It'll wet the public's appetite again. It'll re-open the debate. The way will be cleared. People want their Tazzie tiger back. One press conference about the dismal failure of this expedition, then a sound byte about my proposed cloning project and the letters will pour in. 'Clone the Tazzie Tiger!' they'll say. The Hobart board finally will write me the grant I want to get on with the recovery program. There will be thylacines again, Ellie, but they'll be my thylacines. They'll be bred at the zoo."

"And what'll you do with them, Howard? You won't able to release them. They'll have no pack learn from, no territory, no idea how to hunt for themselves. You think a 'roo mother can do that for them? You want to breed zoo mascots, Howard, not animals that can thrive in the wild."

"Don't be such a purist."

Eleanor squinted, a retort balancing on her tongue, when Goonda stuck his head inside the tent. Under starchy blonde burnished locks, his ever kind, earthy expression stifled her anger. "Rain has let up, so I got a fire going." A big, white grin bloomed on his face. "Supper will be ready in a tick, Eleanor."

Glancing behind him, Goonda noticed the sheen on Mullins's face as he puffed along, stumbling through the sun dappled brush. He smiled. Mullins must have been suffering by now. Unripe bush tomato worked slowly on the gut. The stuff wouldn't kill Mullins, but it would give him intestinal cramps that would double him over by mid morning. Goonda timed the poisoning just so. They would pass Pedder Falls before noon. He was sure that he and Eleanor could talk Mullins into resting there while they went on. Once they left him behind, Goonda could take her to the waldagi den.

He looked forward to where Eleanor paused on an outcrop of rock for a drink from her canteen. She happened to look down trail and noticed Mullins. Her brow crinkled. "Howard , are you alright?"

He puffed. "Bit of a stomach spasm, I'm afraid."

"There's a billabong yonder, Doctor Mullins," Goonda told him, "We could take a smoko."

Panting, Mullins just nodded as he stumbled on. Goonda almost felt sorry for him.

By the time they reached Pedders, Mullins clutched his arms across his middle as he walked. Goonda took pity and shouldered his big pack while Eleanor gathered the cramping Aussie to her side and helped him hobble to a comfortable spot on the bank.

The wide black billabong that spread out beneath a rocky escarpment was fed by a few frothy threads of water that coursed down between towering huon pine and eucalyptus. It was a pretty spot to be sick in.

Mullins eased down on the bank, sagging to the side on one elbow and groaned faintly. "Feels like food poisoning." He eyed Goonda.

The aborigine frowned as he told Eleanor, "could be the bush tomatoes I put in the stew. Some whites don't tolerate them well." Of course, he was telling only half the truth.

"Is it serious?" Eleanor asked.

"He'll be okay, but he should rest, drink water and let the pain pass."

"Howard?"

He sighed, noticing the falls and the water. Some color leaked into his face. "You're sure it'll pass?"

Goonda nodded. "I'm sure."

Mullins sighed. "I guess I'll be here when you get back." He looked around him. "Pretty spot anyway."

They left Mullins behind and headed up slope. Goonda led the way, pretending to read trail sign until he was sure they were out of ear shot of Mullins. Then he turned to Eleanor and told her, "I have something to show you." He pointed above the tree tops along a ridge of rock that was no more than a kilometer up the mountainside. "There." He looked at her lovely blue eyes. "It's a waldagi den, Eleanor."

Her brows pinched. He didn't recognize the expression on her face. It might have been doubt. Her eyes followed the line of his point. She raised her binoculars, fingers adjusting the focus wheels. "How do you know?"

"Because it has always been there."

She lowered the binoculars to squint at him.

"Whites tried to kill off the waldagi once before. Why help them do it again?" Goonda's heart began to pound. He flicked his gaze up slope, suddenly doubtful that he had done the right thing to bring her this far. She was a white. She came to find proof that the waldagi still lived. Maybe he had been fooled by her. He told her, "They need to be protected."

Her squint softened. "Of course." Then she said, "But why bring me here if you don't trust whites?"

"Because I think you are like us, like the people of the Dreaming. I think you understand the way things must be." Goonda looked up slope. He began to think he made a mistake. Whether he did or not, it no longer mattered. She was here. Whether he took her to the den or not, it didn't matter. She could find her way back and she would bring others. Committed now, Goonda started up slope. "Come."

Soft yips rose through the bush. The sound made Eleanor's hackles prickle erect. Mullins let her listen to the recordings the zoo made of the last few thylacines they held in captivity in the 1930s. The sound was unmistakable. As her heart began to pound, Eleanor slipped the straps of her backpack from her shoulders, pushed back the flap and slipped out the tranquilizer gun, checked the cartridges in the barrel, and flicked the safety off.

Treading on their toes, they crept up over moss carpeted slope. A steep wall of rock rose on the left, the bush thinned on the right as the mountainside dropped away to the tree tops of the pine and eucalypt forest below.

Ahead of her, Goonda pressed back the last of the thicket and nodded, "There."

Eleanor raised her dart gun to look down the sight.

In the cross hairs of her scope, a cluster of agile, cat like bodies moved liquidly around a small carcass in the mouth of the cave. About the size of a German Shepherd Dog, their tight, muscular, crisply striped haunches lunged and jerked as they tore meat off their most recent kill. With delighted viciousness, two adults grasped opposite ends of the wallaby in their powerful jaws and shook their heads violently, tearing off chunks of flesh. It made Eleanor think of the time she clung to her father's leg while his crew filmed a pack of African wild dogs mauling a Thompson's Gazelle fawn. Unlike the dogs, there was no growling, or barking, just the eerie, muffled crunching of their raw lunch.

One of the thylacines lifted its long, fox like head. Muzzle covered in blood, it sniffed at the air. It looked straight at Eleanor. After staring for a moment, it gave a yip.

She cursed under her breath, trying to sight one of the females passed Goonda's shoulder.

All the other heads snapped up. Bloody muzzles all twisted toward Eleanor and Goonda. Pups instinctively dove between their mothers' legs into their pouches.

Cross hairs centering on between stripes on a muscular haunch, Eleanor held her breath and squeezed the trigger.

The *pop!* of the gun made Goonda twist. In that split second of reaction, Eleanor saw his brown face blanch and his eyes flare in terror. He thought she was shooting the animals. He slapped the pistol out of her hand and shoved her back.

Loose shale rolled like marbles beneath her boots. Eleanor slipped, going down hard on her stomach. As she slid off the side of the steep cliff side trail, she glimpsed the pack dashing away from the den sight, into the woods at the far edge of the little plateau; a field of bobbing striped rumps that dissolved instantly into the greenery. An instant later the world rolled into a tumbling blur of green and tan. It all rushed by. Eleanor clawed at the cliff side as momentum dragged her passed branches and roots, making her miss the first few opportunities for hand holds. They whipped her hands, cutting her palms. Sliding, sensing the edge coming up too fast, she ignored the gravel rasping her belly where her jacket and shirt pulled up, and dug her boots into the loose slag of the slope to try to save herself. Fingers raked the rock and dirt. Her nails peeled back to the quick, but she started to slow. More bush swept passed her. Eleanor's hand shot out instinctively. She caught hold of a single eucalyptus sapling and snapped to a halt. Her shoulder wrenched, but the little tree held firm. Adrenalin stalling for a moment, Eleanor puffed against the dirt, catching whiffs of moist turf and stone as she worked the treads of her boots into the ledge. Her left one briefly toed naked air until the tread caught hold of the rock . It gave her a queasy feeling. If she hadn't grabbed that sapling ….

Boots planted, she pushed herself up the steep grade. She tested fresh hands holds to make sure the roots didn't tear loose when she pulled herself up. Pebbles rolled passed her head. Resting a moment, Eleanor looked up along the muddy, stony path her body just cut through the bushy slope, she cursed softly. She slid further than she thought. "Goonda!" He didn't answer. She shouted, "I need help."

His silhouette appeared against the sky. "I'm sorry, Eleanor."

Cursing, Eleanor hauled herself up, hooking her elbow around a bigger sapling. She dug her treads into the slag again and rested. "I wasn't trying to kill them, Goonda. It was a tranquilizer gun."

"I know, but I can't let you take them." He drew back, disappearing from the ledge. "They belong here."

"Goonda." Eleanor cursed. "Goonda!"

Goonda left her on the cliff side. Eleanor had a good grip, so he was sure she wouldn't fall. He would go back for her. He didn't mean to push her off the trail. As much as he wanted to protect the waldagi, he was not a murderer. He only meant to knock her back, to divert her shot, but he wasn't quick enough.

He found one waldagi on the ground. Her breaths rose and fell evenly under her coat of short, tan fur. He plucked the dart from her striped hip. Her hind legs jiggled oddly as her pup wriggled half way out the pouch to look at him. Its brown eyes showed no fear. It snuffled the air, damp nostrils wafting his scent.

He crouched and spoke softly to it in his native tongue. "It's alright, little brother." Then he leaned toward the female's head. Her long gape was slightly open. She panted. Her tongue lolled out and was powdered with dirt from where it brushed the ground. Her eyes were open, too. One dilated pupil fixed on him. "Wake up, Mother. Wake up." He pinched her ear, but she didn't move. He frowned. Too much of the drug had gotten into her blood. He knew enough about darting to know that she would be down for at least a half an hour. He didn't want to leave Eleanor clinging to the side of the cliff that long. He just needed enough time to rouse the animal so it could stagger off into the bush. No doubt Eleanor meant to call in a chopper to lift the waldagi and her pup off the mountain, so that they could spend their lives in crates and pens. He couldn't let that happen. They were better off here. Maybe Eleanor had stimulants as well as tranquilizers in her pack. He turned toward the trail to look for it.

Mullins stood there holding the pack in one hand and a gun in the other. At first, Goonda thought it was Eleanor's tranq gun then he realized it was heavier and larger. The little hairs on the aborigine's arms prickled erect.

Bent over his cramping gut, Mullins snickered, "what's this then?" He pointed the weapon while he looked over the waldagi and her pup. He looked a long time, huffed and gave his head a shake. "Ellie was right." He blinked, glancing around the den site. "Where is she, Goonda?"

"It was an accident. I pushed her. She fell -"

Mullins glanced behind him, at the bush filled ledge. "Criky! You killed her?"

"No! She —"

"You crazy abo. I bet you tried to poison me, didn't you?"

"She's not dead, Doctor. She's got a hold on the side of the mountain just there. Have a look."

Mullins chuckled, not taking his eyes off Goonda. He must have thought it was a trick. He waved the muzzle, "Step aside."

"You don't need to use that."

"And I won't if you just step aside."

"I can't do that, Doctor. The waldagi belongs here."

"You fool. We can breed them much faster at the zoo and release them back to the wild."

"It's not Sun Mother's way."

Mullins snorted, "Abo nonsense. Now. Move."

Goonda stood straighter and braced his feet. "No."

Mullins cursed under his breath. For a moment, his expression softened. Goonda thought he was loosing his resolve then the light in the Aussie's eyes shifted. He raised the pistol. His stare cooled. He growled, "move."

Goonda braced again.

"Now!" Mullins eyes darted. "Now!"

Goonda shirked, but held his ground. He didn't understand until he saw the gun shift its aim passed him. He never heard the animals coming, only felt the impact drive him to the ground. Jaws clamped down like a vice on his nape. He curled into a ball instantly, trying to protect his head and neck. Mullins's revolver started popping. The waldagi yelped as they were hit. Goonda screamed, "no!" at Mullins. He screamed, "no!" from the ungodly force of those jaws tearing muscle from bone. He screamed, "no!" because it was all going so horribly wrong.

When the last set of jaws sprang free, he rolled away from their agony wracked, dying whimpers. Mullins grabbed him by the arm and dragged him clear.

Hardly able to turn his head, Goonda looked back at the animals' bodies sprawled in the dirt. One still struggled to rise, trying to roll up onto its paralyzed hind legs. Mullins stepped up to it with his weapon.

"No...." Goonda whimpered, though he knew there was no other choice now.

The big male twisted toward Mullins and snapped. The Aussie aimed and shot it in the head. It dropped like a rag doll.

Goonda's beloved waldagi lay scattered across their den floor. Half the pack was massacred. When the Aussi looked at him, Goonda saw regret in his eyes, too. It was too much. Guilt and shock spun Goonda's consciousness but ....

He shook himself alert, eyes burning, vision blurred. They watered painfully as he squeezed them tightly closed. He remembered his mauled neck and wiped a hand over his wet nape. Blinking his vision clear, he saw that his fingers came away with water, not blood. He looked around him. The fire dreaming burned away with the steam rising from the pot boiling on the sterno. In the dark, he looked toward the glistening tent. It was lit from within. He could hear Mullins and Eleanor arguing gently.

"No more valid than those of Bigfoot...." Mullins said.

Goonda looked around him.

They were still down slope of Federation Peak, still a day's walk form the den site and a day's walk from all that was yet to happen.

Goonda looked down. A handkerchief full of bush tomatoes lay at his feet. The poisonous green ones were separated from the ripe red ones. He stared at them a moment, separating out the fruits of his dreaming from those of reality so that he might reckon what was to be and what could be changed.

After a moment, Goonda smiled.

Sun Mother was wise.

He picked up the unripe bush tomatoes and pitched them into the brush. He wouldn't need them now. The trail was mud. The rain washed away all traces of the waldagi pack. As far as Goonda was concerned he had lost the track. He wouldn't find it again. Eleanor would be disappointed, but thanks to Sun Mother, he dream walked the future and saw the cunning American through her very own eyes and she was not what desire told him she would be. Yet, she would still get what she wanted. They all would.

Let the white man dream the waldagi back to life with science. The aborigine will dream it back to life with nature.

Either way, the waldagi wins.

BAKU AND THE DREAM CATCHERS

Suds washed down Taiko's throat like cold sand. Over the lip of his beer glass, he eyed the mirror hung on the wall behind the bar. It reflected the tables behind him. A woman had been watching him for the better part of an hour. Long black hair. Almond eyes. Attractive. He thought she might be Japanese. She sat alone.

Maybe he wasn't drunk enough, or maybe the old dream eater had sucked too much of the life out of him, but he still hadn't decided whether to approach her. He just didn't care enough about getting laid to make the effort. He hadn't barhopped in years and he only came to O'Leary's tonight to celebrate a private anniversary. Although this year, the beer buzz didn't feel like much. He sighed.

Everything was going to slip away from him just like it did for his father. One day he might even take the old Buick and drive it off a cliff just like Dad did. He dropped his gaze from the mirror to the soapy scum in his empty glass. His sodden brain swam into the past and the mistake his father didn't live long enough to warn him about.

Taiko was six.

Something woke him out of a sound sleep. He wasn't aware of hearing a sound, but the feeling of a presence lasted. He opened his eyes and saw it leaning halfway out of his closet. It paused, then raised its head into the banded moonlight coming through the blinds, revealing a milky eye. The whiskers on its muzzle sparkled like spun glass in the full moon. It gave a couple of short, sharp sniffs then stepped toward the bed.

Skin pimpling, bladder muscles twisting tight against a new surge of fear, Taiko sank into his mattress. He tried to hide as he peeped out from under his covers. The creature ran its pale eyes over the bed to the hoop hung over his headboard.

In the slashes of moonlight leaking through the blinds, he saw that its body was like that of a starving lion, except that it was easily able to balance on its hind legs. It held itself erect. Looking up at its chin, it looked just like a lion above the shoulders. It was white, like clouds, almost pretty, if not for its black mouth and gleaming black teeth, the huge canines poking out from under its lips.

It grunted, like his grandfather used to when he approved of something, leaned toward the hoop, and sniffed again. Its lip curled, revealing glossy black gums.

"Another one," it growled in a baritone of such resonance that the vibration rolled through Taiko. The bones in his arms and legs hummed.

The creature leaned forward, its mane brushing across Taiko's pillow as it nimbly caught the hoop on a heavily clawed forepaw and pulled it from the wall. It eased back on its haunches as it turned the hoop back and forth, studying it intently. It toyed with the feather tassels, batting them with finesse, completely absorbed. Without looking up, it said, "I know that you are awake, Taiko."

Taiko nearly peed in his bed. Too terrified to speak, let alone reckon how the thing knew his name, he shrunk deeper into his blankets.

"Yes, I know your name just as I know your thoughts. You may call me Baku as so many others do." Those moon-bright eyes blinked slowly. "I knew your father, too. He was of great service to me. Now that he is gone, I need another to replace him."

Taiko blinked. He and his mother buried his father on Monday. She told him that there was a car accident, but at the wake someone whispered, "suicide."

Baku shifted forward on his haunches. "Hmmm. You could be of service to me, too. Your father didn't tell you about the spirit beings of his people, did he?" Its nostrils flared a moment. "No matter. You carry the scent of your father's people."

Baku cocked its head, thick mane sparkling. "You may have been borne in this land, but you have Nipponese blood and that is enough."

Taiko swallowed.

Baku sniffed at the hoop, moaned favorably and said, "Ripe nightmares." It eyed Taiko, "You dream about the funeral, don't you? You dream about the people crying. You dream about your father rising bloody and groaning from the casket. You think he's in terrible pain when you dream of him like that. Such dread sights in the light give you dread dreams in the dark."

Taiko shrugged, holding himself with both hands under his covers to keep from peeing in fright, too scared even to shout for his mother, afraid Baku would hurt her.

It looked him over. "Would you like the nightmares to go away forever?"

Those moon-white eyes captured him as he nodded slowly.

Baku smiled. "Very well then." It paused a moment to lick the twine webbing stretched across the hoop of the dream catcher, seemed to mull the flavor a moment and noticed Taiko again.

It held out the hoop. "Let's see if you have the gift. Smell this."

Limbs still rubbery, but beginning to lose the edge of his terror, Taiko sat up and sniffed at the dream catcher.

"What's it smell like?"

Taiko stammered, "Stinks."

"Like sulfur?"

Taiko shrugged, not sure what sulfur smelled like.

"Like rotten eggs?"

Taiko nodded.

"Good boy. That's what burned dreams smell like. You have the nose for the work."

"What work?"

Baku grinned in black.

Years later, Taiko was still stealing nightmares for the old demon. Together, they spared little children the ravages of night terrors. The crafty old dream eater charmed him, making him believe in the cause for years without realizing all that the work was taking from him. The changes happened so slowly that Taiko didn't notice until it was too late. All he knew was that after he met Baku, the colors in life's joys bled away.

With them went his ambitions and his hopes. He barely finished high school. He never finished college. He drifted from job to job, but all along he served Baku. Even the pastel memories of long-forsaken dreams rarely drifted up into his thoughts anymore.

Taiko never dreamed, never nightmared. He began to catch snapshot-like moments of his father in himself. Life became a monotonous, perpetual conveyor belt of days. The matter of putting one foot in front of the other became a dull, dead habit.

Even creeping into people's houses to steal their hoops full of nightmares no longer thrilled him. Taiko began to hate the gray predictability of it, but he couldn't stop. He was afraid to stop. The grayness of the hunt was the only shade of life left him. Without it there was only darkness.

A touch startled him.

Slender fingers curled gently around Taiko's biceps. He looked up into brown eyes as warm and dark and deep as Baku's were cold and white and shallow.

She smiled. It was the woman who had been watching him all night.

"My name is Asibikaashi," she shouted over the throbbing base of the jukebox. "You can call me Kaashi."

"Taiko." He looked her over. "Japanese-American?"

Brown eyes fixed upon him. She shook her head. A few strands of black spilled over her shoulder like ink. "No, Ojibwe tribe."

Charmed, Taiko tried to flatter her, "Oh, a Native American."

The twinkle in her dark eyes vanished. She leaned in and insisted, "No. Ojibwe."

Taiko envied her passion. He hadn't felt anything like it in years. He apologized for his insensitivity. Her smile returned as her fingers tightened on his arm. She tipped her head so that her full lips brushed Taiko's ear. Tingling washed across his face, down his nape and his shoulders, then spilled into his soul and parts south. The noise in the bar drained away.

She said, "I know what the old dream eater did to you."

Taiko pulled back to stare at her, not quite believing what he heard. How could she know? How could anybody know? How could anyone believe what happened to him? Yet Kaashi even knew the species of the old demon that spelled him all those years ago.

"How...?"

Her smile grew. Her dark gaze roamed over his face, somehow imperious and compassionate at the same time.

"The Ojibwe, my children, are the people of the dream weavers, Taiko. We know all the creatures of the twilight that trouble the web of dreams. The one who spelled you is especially bothersome to me. He is as a moth on the tapestry of life, endlessly devouring the tender threads of light and dark until there is nothing left."

Taiko looked at her carefully. She talked like Baku did, but there was something more about her. Maybe he had lived in Baku's presence long enough that he developed a sense for the ethereal beings that existed, for the most part, outside of the human scope of experience.

He realized that it was more than the way she talked. It was the air around her. Kaashi was familiar, and yet...not.

Taiko guessed, "You're a demon like him."

She huffed, apparently charmed, and gave her head a gentle shake. "No. I'm much more." She leaned close again and breathed, "I am that which weaves the dreams your master eats. I am the mother spider of the dream weaver people and I know how to set you free."

Fingers digging into the armrest, Taiko slid against the passenger's side door as the old Buick took the tight curve of the exit ramp too fast. Kaashi's gourd rattle, hung from the rear view mirror, swayed and jiggled the pea gravel inside it. The stones hissed as they chafed the belly of the rattle.

As the car rattled down the ramp onto the Northway, Taiko noticed the speedometer as the needle climbed passed sixty-five.

"Better keep to the speed limit."

Kaashi tossed her head, flipping back a silky, black lock. Her brown eyes flicked at him.

"We won't crash, Taiko."

"It's not that. It's cops."

He nodded toward the backseat. It was filled to the ceiling with a tangle of willow hoops, feathers, and beads that clacked together from the vibration of the speeding car. They had broken into a strip mall gift shop near the bar and cleaned out the stockroom. Kaashi had insisted on taking all the dream catchers off the walls in the display room as well. Taiko hadn't thought it was necessary, but she had said that they would need all of them.

"If we get stopped for speeding, they'll want to know where we got those."

"At two in the morning, Taiko?"

"There'll still be troopers on the road."

She nodded, frowning a little. "Of course." The needle on the speedometer slid back to sixty-four. She twitched off a smile.

Taiko eyed her. She seemed a little over eager. "You're going to like killing it, aren't you?"

"Aren't you? Look what Baku did to your life, to your father's life."

Even after everything that had happened, Taiko wasn't sure. He had been used, his dreams bled away. He had lost his father to Baku's appetite and, yet, he didn't relish destroying the old dream eater. Not like Kaashi did. Maybe he'd lost the capacity for vengeance, the same as he had lost the capacity to feel just about everything else.

"What are you ... mortal enemies or something?"

"Mortal? No, but Baku's kind of gluttony is ruining the world. Look around you. Has there ever been more despair, more hopelessness and fear? People need to dream, Taiko."

"So you're here to set things right?"

She shrugged her pencil-thin black brows. "I've been freeing his harvesters one-by-one for centuries." She flicked off her smile a second time as she watched the road.

"You're the last one," she said.

Taiko looked out the window to watch the business district drop away in clumps. She was lovely and wise and, of course, she was right, but he wondered whether her plan would work.

"It'll work. Trust me."

Taiko shrugged down in his seat, annoyed that she seemed to know what was going on inside his head. He fixed his gaze out the window, off the side of the road. The bundles of artless, gray, cinder block buildings with that lowbrow, flat-roofed look gradually broke up as they traveled north. The countryside slowly invaded, divided, and swallowed civilization with trees. Two hundred year old hemlocks, white pines, and oaks filled the dark, rolling slopes of the Adirondacks.

Taiko rolled the window down. As gray as the world had become, the air here was still filled with sweet, green scents.

The first exit sign for Lake George flashed by. Albany long gone, lurking somewhere an hour south in the dark, Taiko's shoulders dropped. If the cops hadn't pulled them over yet, they weren't going to. They were home free.

He glanced into the dark back seat. Beads glittered. Feathers fluttered as the wind cut through his open window. He picked up one of the hoops and sniffed at it.

"They smell different than ones people have dreamed into," he said.

Kaashi shrugged. "But they smell like something, Taiko. That's all we need."

He sniffed again. The catchers weren't bitter smelling, but they did carry the tang of irritable thoughts. Angry customers, bored and frustrated store clerks, a colicky, bawling baby; all hard smells borne from bitter moods. But they weren't dreams--or nightmares, Baku's favorite food.

"I don't think it'll be fooled."

"You're worrying too much."

"What if it can tell the difference?"

Turning the wheel to guide the Buick onto the exit ramp, Kaashi told him, "It can't."

The car rolled through the village, passed the marinas, dark T-shirt shops, and restaurants and then headed up 9L, weaving along the lake. The water sparkled in the waning moonlight like Baku's hoary mane.

Taiko put the hoop back as the Buick slowed to make the turn into the long driveway of the old house he rented. Baku liked the roomy closets there.

Kaashi said, "With no others feeding it, old dream eater is the weakest it has ever been. Those tainted dream catchers will finish it off. Then, Taiko, you'll be free."

He felt a chill. Fear. It was the first time he felt fear in years. It felt good. It also felt bad.

"What do we do after?"

Kaashi didn't answer while she pulled up to the garage, clicked the opener on the dash and watched the door lift. Maybe she didn't know. Maybe they would know after. Maybe it didn't matter. Taiko wasn't free yet.

The Buick rolled in, wheels crackling softly over the grit on the floor, and stopped. Kaashi flicked the headlights off. For a moment they sat in the dark. It was pure and thick and made Taiko think of what life would feel like without the gray glimmer of the hunt, his last and only purpose in life.

He lost courage. "I don't know."

"Don't give up now, Taiko. We're almost there. Just because you can't imagine tomorrow without Baku, doesn't mean it won't come."

He couldn't help it. He stared at the dark. He tried to see tomorrow, tried to see the color of it. He couldn't. There was just oblivion. No being. Nonexistence.

Nothing.

"Taiko."

He startled and looked at Kaashi. Her pretty oval face filled his consciousness. How could she be so placid at a moment like this? When she smiled, his soul gulped down a sweet drop of hope. It seemed to flash in the dark. And when she pressed her warm, dry mouth against his, he saw a little more light. He could almost see tomorrow without Baku. The sparkle there. The hope.

She drew back, dark lashes drooping as she looked at his mouth then raised her dark eyes. The confidence there plumbed all the way to her ageless soul.

Bewitched, Taiko caught himself murmuring, "Asibikaashi." In just the few hours since he'd met her, he found himself more entangled in her web than in Baku's. He was glad of it.

The queen of the dream weaver people smiled and touched his cheek.

"Grab those catchers."

Taiko popped the lock on the rear passenger's side door then gathered all the hoops in his arms. Kaashi opened the door to the kitchen for him. His arms full, he carried the dream catchers up the backstairs to the second floor. He dropped a couple on the way up, but heard Kaashi say, "I've got them," as she made progress up the creaking tread behind him.

On the landing, Taiko paused to glance over his shoulder. "I have a spare room where it likes to appear."

Kaashi nodded.

He padded over the hardwood. Baku liked to enter from the big closet with the double doors. As Taiko stepped inside, Kaashi flicked the switch behind him. The bedroom lit up. It was bare except for rows of nails that studded the walls.

They began hanging the dream catchers. The flicker of fear he felt in the car returned. Only it was bigger now and shook him from the inside out. Taiko's hands began to tremble.

Kaashi leaned close. "We're going to make it."

Though he nodded, Taiko swallowed a knot of dread. He just couldn't see tomorrow happening. He simply couldn't imagine it without Baku.

"Taiko," Kaashi said, folding a hand over his cold fingers.

He looked at her. She nodded at the closet doors. The left one shifted.

Baku baritoned from behind the door, "They smell strange."

"It was all I could find," Taiko lied, "but there's a lot of them."

The closet doors remained patient and quiet.

"Let's finish up." Kaashi whispered.

They hung the rest of the catchers, then turned out the light and closed the door to the spare room. They listened only a moment, hearing Baku shuffle across the floor. After a moment of quiet, they began to hear crunching.

Though the sounds filled Taiko with subtle terror, he noticed a little smile bloom on Kaashi's face. She took his hand and led him off to bed. While Baku munched circle after circle of poisonous emptiness at the other end of the house, they kissed and touched the anxieties away until Taiko turned his eager spider mother on her back in his bed and took her, his rhythm building from tender gratitude to ferocious abandon. For a few explosive minutes, he lost his fear of facing tomorrow without Baku.

For precious seconds, caught tight inside Kaashi, Taiko didn't care if tomorrow never came.

But it did.

In the quiet of sun-splashed sheets, Taiko gazed at Kaashi's prim, golden breasts and golden torso and tried to feel the change. Sleepy and peaceful, he noticed the way the sun cast twinkling beams through the dust suspended in the air.

He thought of Baku, rolled out of bed, pulled up his sweat pants, and padded barefoot down the hall. Cracking open the door to the spare room, Taiko found the light was just the same there, sparkling and serene. The wall, tangled with hoops and feathers and beads last night, was now empty of everything but the nails. It was strangely quiet, like a graveyard.

He stepped in, noticing fragments of Baku's last meal. A bead here, a feather there. Shards of willow lay scattered across the pine flooring.

Taiko noticed the closet and swallowed heavily. He stepped to it and opened the left door. A tiny draft stirred up a whirling dust devil; a tiny, silvery twister that quickly disintegrated into a considerable mound of glittering talc. Taiko crouched, scooping up a handful of the pearlescent dust. It reminded him of the full moon glittering on whiskers like spun glass and dark teeth that gleamed like obsidian.

He held it to his nose and sniffed. All the horrors were there. The sulfur of every child's terror: monsters under the bed, boogeymen in the closet, the green-teethed goblins and movie menaces that skulked through little frightened minds at night.

Now that Baku was gone, there was nothing to eat those terrors.

"Oh God," Taiko said, realizing what they had done. Who would eat all the night terrors now? Who would be there to rescue children from their own horrific imaginations in the dark? The oblivion Taiko feared so much, he had visited on the old lion-faced dream eater instead. What a mistake! He picked up Baku's silvery ashes, letting them run through his numb fingers. What a horrible mistake. His heart sank.

And yet...

He noticed a smell in the closet; something like honey and apple blossoms. It was sweet and wholesome. He sniffed Baku's dust again. The heady aroma of all that night terror surprised him. Without knowing why, he lifted the handful to his lips. He tasted it.

Never did anything taste so sweet, so delicious. He sipped the dead dream eater's ashes and realized that this was what Baku savored when he licked at the strings of the catchers. This is what the minor gods eat for sustenance. What a service! What a great kindness! How they must treasure the pure hearts of children to lick away the dirt and spurn of their imaginations.

He noticed the back of the closet. The wall began to change, turning mildly vaporous. The moment of his strange Eucharist altered his senses.

He stared at it uncertain, but curiosity began to build momentum.

"Taiko?" Kaashi called from the bedroom.

Taiko felt heat come up in his cheeks as he clapped his hands, scattering the precious talc. He looked over his shoulder. The room was bright with life and thoughts and being. He could see today. He could see tomorrow. He could see every dream and hope and aspiration humankind ever had and would ever have. Glorious, white, sparkling thoughts. No wonder Baku ate nightmares. The wonder that remained was breathtaking.

He looked at the back of the closet again. The wall was gone. The way out opened. He glimpsed Baku's kingdom waiting there.

"Taiko?" Kaashi sounded like she was getting up. Hers was the voice of the queen spider of dreams, the spinner mother of all the dream demons and angels.

He began scooping handfuls of sweet dust, shoveling it into his mouth. He didn't swallow. The ashes melted away like cotton candy. Their essence flowed into his very being.

He crouched low and dragged his tongue through the last of the dust, licking up every last grain. He wanted all of Baku inside him. He didn't want to leave a bit of the dream eater behind. He couldn't.

"Taiko? Where are you?" She was in the hall.

The spectacle unfolded before Taiko, filling him with the bliss of purpose. Baku was dead, but it lived, too.

He stepped into the closet.

"Taiko?"

As the queen of the dream weavers opened the door to the bedroom, the new king of the dream eaters closed the closet door behind him and slipped away.

First published in *Mytholog*, March 2003.

DUPE

Teddi waited in the reception module, seated on one of the blue plastic chairs that lined the observation window. She gazed outside watching a pale shuttle float in like a paper air plane through Chijini's piercing blue, absolutely cloudless sky. Her tan, slender legs were crossed at the knees. Her left sandal hung off her suspended foot almost ready to slip off her toes. In the sun-drenched window, her long hair glowed like molten gold. She had thick, shaggy bangs, like the forelock of a sexy pony.

I watched her a moment longer before I said, "Ted."

She looked over. Expression sedated with boredom, the spray of freckles beneath her pale eyes made her look innocently eight, not twenty-eight, then her grin bloomed with a hint of blushing embarrassment. "William. You're early!"

Deliciously agile, she jumped up and rushed to me, brown arms folding tight around my neck. Her lean body pressed tight, precisely fitting the empty mold that lingered in my memory. She kissed hard in her excitement, bruising my lip, but I didn't mind.

"God. You're so solid. So real. I can't believe the scanning pods actually work."

I chuckled, feeling everything work as I cupped her ass and crushed her against me. "Better than laying in cryo for six or seven months."

She giggled, pretty teeth flashing again as she leaned in back in my arms, keeping her flat belly pressed against me. *Umph*. Her gaze sparkled as she looked me over. There was such glee, such anticipation there. I forgot how insanely vivacious Teddi was. Loving her was like looking at the sun too long. Her energy could blind a man if he wasn't careful. If anyone belonged on Chijini, it was Teddi Benders.

Her grin faded. "God. But it's not really real is it? It's not like you're really here. William's still back on Earth. You're just … just … well, a copy. Isn't that how it works?"

That hurt a little, but I was too happy to have her there, clamped against me to be bothered much. So I quirked a brow and told her, "I'm there and I'm here, too, Babe." I patted her firm fanny. "The real me is on Earth, but the real me is here, too. I got the same genes, same cells, same memories, same everything. It's still me. I'm here and I'm real."

She squinted, then giggled and hugged me again. "Well, it doesn't matter anyway."

Catching a whiff of her citrus scented shampoo once more, I squeezed her toned rear and thought exactly the same thing.

Teddi grabbed my hand and pulled me away from the threshold. "Come on. You're going to love it here."She hurried me through the spaceport. "It's Paradise, William. Once you see it, you'll want to come for real. You'll want to stay."

Beyond the huge tinted windows, people began deplaning onto the glittering white tarmac. They all wore dark eye films that make them look like bugs. Drawn, pale faces and stiff gaits told me that they had been aboard a cryoship for a good part of the trip and a superlumer for the rest. My duped molecules cringed at the idea. Seven months. They spent seven months gliding through the blackest, emptiest reaches of space, dipping in and out of cryo throughout the trip.

As for me? I never felt a thing. I stepped naked from the transition room scanner at Kennedy and stepped out the other side into the transition room of my destination. I was a little woozy but an attendant there guided me over to a recovery cell. Once my blood pressure and heart rate stabilized, she brought me a robe and showed me to the locker room where the clothing I ordered for the trip was already waiting in my locker. The whole process lasted all of forty minutes. I only lost thirty minutes of consciousness. Hell, I signed the insurance waiver without reading it.

I sent 'me' here to dump Teddi. I planned to enjoy her brown, firm beach bunny body for a week and then make the end something coarse and ugly, something that would leave no doubt in her mind that I was done with her.

When she signed onto colonize Chinjini I was glad to be rid of her, but she nagged me to go with her for weeks before she left. Then after she got there, the damned postcards started coming and they wouldn't stop. So, I sent myself ahead to 'Dear Jane' her, but ...

Now that I was here, now that I saw her again... I don't know. Maybe I don't have to be so rough. Maybe we could have some fun. I could let her down easy. Teddi was reasonable. Teddi was sweet. She just wanted me with her. That's all.

It's flattering really.

I glimpsed at my watch. It was still set to New York time. Nine-fifteen in the morning. I had been at the office a couple of hours already, was probably pouring my third cup of coffee and snickering about how things were going here.

Or, was I?

After all, I wasn't the same man any more. The moment I stepped out of the scanner, William Masters and I diverged. I'm having experiences and thoughts William isn't. Maybe Teddi was right in a sense. I wasn't the man who stepped into the scanner. Now that I thought of it, I don't feel the way I remember him feeling; stiff inside his own skin. Smug. Ambitious. He's a bastard, really.

Nope. I wasn't William. I was ... Will. Yes. Will. That felt right. I looked at Teddi again.

What was he thinking? She's beautiful. She's fun.

She dazzled me. How could William miss that? He must have exorcized all his passion all in the scanner. Maybe I got it all. The passion he felt when he first met her, I felt now. What a weird feeling.

What a weird, fantastic feeling.

I grinned as Teddi pulled me along. Maybe it was just the vacationing sort of mood I was in, but I began to believe I left behind the manic, corporate giant killer part of me back on Earth. God, I felt sorry for that poor bastard. What the hell is he breaking his back for?

I adored Teddi Benders. I lusted after Teddi Benders and I was glad of it.

She led me outside into the sun. The tarmac glowed like snow in a spot light, flashing too bright for my eyes. The light stabbed my retinas. "Sheesh." I couldn't cover them fast enough. They watered painfully in the red-dark of my bent arm.

"Almost forgot." Teddi said, pulling at the arm I used to cover my tearing eyes.

I chanced a look. The brilliance pulsed.

She pulled a pair of sleek little sun glasses from the straw bag hanging from her arm. "You'll need these for a while."

The relief was instant. The smartspecs molded themselves to my face sealing out the harshest reflections off that snow bright tarmac, yet kept a faint enough tint that I didn't notice any change in the colors of the landscape at all.

Beyond the port, Kai Island was white coral sands and tropical paradise. Palmetto, plantain, coconut …. It looked like the resort planners imported every terran tropical fruit tree that would grow in this environment.

"No wonder you left Earth."

Teddi nodded vigorously, "great, huh! I'm so glad I made the trip. It was worth it." She tugged me toward a parking lot full two-seater buggies with big, slender solar fins on their roofs.

Chattering all the way, Teddi drove us back to her bungalow along the coast highway. The vista of pale sand and gently swelling turquoise shallows rolled passed us like it was on a perpetual conveyor belt.

Apparently, there was a lot to do on the island and Teddi planned to pack it all into my seven day visa.

I watched her drive, remembering the day she asked William go with her a year ago. He laughed. He thought she was being ridiculous. She was just another piece of pretty ass. "My life is here." He said.

Suits. Tight shoes. Endless droning meetings. It's like communing with the undead day after day. The smell of bum's piss in the subway on a humid summer day. What the hell was he talking about? What life?

I lifted a hand to the hibiscus scented breeze flowing over the sun buggy and admired the way the sun bounced off Teddi's nut brown skin. "Living in paradise. What in God's name made me say 'no'."

She took a hand off the wheel to squeeze my knee. "You can always change your mind."

"My visa expires in one week, Babe." Temptation tickled me in a couple of places. "I suppose I could ignore it."

"You can't do that."

"Not legally, you mean."

"You could sign colonization papers. You could come for real, not just send a –" she caught herself.

"-A dupe," I laughed.

She blushed. "I'm sorry."

"Teddi, I am William." No I was better than that. He was a drudge. A moron. I was lighter. I was happier than that. "I'm Will. In the flesh. Want me to prove it?" I leaned toward her for a grope. Teddi growled playfully, sticking her sharp elbow in my chest. "I'm driving you fool."

I sank back in my seat and noticed the ocean. Turquoise gave way to piercing indigo depths. Deep sea fishing here could be interesting. Who knows what was swimming around out there. The waves rose and crashed into curls of vanilla foam. "Maybe I'll just go AWOL."

"Dupes can't do that, William. You shouldn't even joke about it."

I shrugged. Maybe it was the sea air and the fragrance of hibiscus, but the fantasy of never stepping back into the scanner appealed to me. Maybe it was just the idea that Teddi said that I couldn't do it that made me want to do it. After all, the scanner would just blow away my duped atoms and transfer my experience back into William's body. I'd be back in his skin shackled to his mindless ambition.

Who knows, maybe I wouldn't mind. Maybe I'd never remember how I felt being Will.

Not too appealing.

The finger of oblivion tickled my freshly minted soul. That strange, sinking terror of unbeing clung to my consciousness. I shook it off.

To distract myself, I asked, "What else are we doing?"

She must have been thinking in terms of negatives now because she said, "the only thing we won't do this week is wind surf." She taught wind surfing at the resort.

I laughed. "No problem." After all, Teddi was on vacation, too. "So where do you want to go for lunch?"

"It's dinner time here."

Even better. "So, where do you want to go for dinner?"

Her sly smile struck me as a double entendre. I was wrong. Sort of.

The trilobite – or at least, that's what it looked like - that the waiter brought to our table was the size of a turkey. Presented on its back the segments cooked to a bright orange just like lobster. Its legs were folded over a hot, glazed marinade of coconut, pineapple and meat mounded up in the middle of the scraped out shell. A couple of hibiscus flowers had been stuck in the center. It was like some sort of cretaceous Polynesian delicacy. Creamy steam curled up off the dish. Tangy-sweet, it made my mouth water.

Teddi reached over and snapped off a leg that was twice the size of a drumstick as she told me, "tastes like crab." She went to work cracking the shell and prying out the pale meat inside with a fork.

Still amazed at the size of the thing, I noticed it had a long, spiny tail and touched it.

Teddi brushed my arm with juicy fingers. She winked. "Save that for last. They say the meat inside the tail is an aphrodisiac."

I chuckled, broke off a leg and picked up my fork. "Then you eat it, 'cause I won't need it."

Teddi laughed, pretty teeth flashing in the dark. Coconut marinade dribbled whitely down her chin. I dabbed it off. Ya gotta love her.

Then, out the blue, she said, "so why didn't you ship out with me?"

I remembered William gritting his teeth at the walltall in his office; his inbox full of video postcards from Teddi. I couldn't tell her that

William thought she was a vapid twit and he wanted her to disappear, so I shrugged a shoulder. "I guess I wanted the brass ring."

She blinked, "what do you want now?"

"You."

She wrinkled her brow then giggled.

You can't imagine how good that giggle felt. I kissed her coconutty chin. She let herself drift into the kiss, just barely and broke off. Her pale eyes flicked away, looking out at dark beach. The glow of the tikis made her eyes luminous. Out there two dusky figures, lovers probably, strolled hand in hand along the edge of the florescent tide. As quick as I had her, I lost her again.

She watched the lovers the way a cat watches mice. "I don't understand why William didn't come himself."

I gritted my teeth, then relaxed, and picked up her hand a kissed off the coconut juice there. "But he did come, Teddi. I'm him. Only better because I want to be here."

"And William doesn't?"

I didn't mean for it to come out that way, so I said, "Because he can't."

"But you can make him want to come to Chijini. Won't he pick up the mnemes from the trip when you return to the scanner?"

He would, but he wouldn't absorb my passion for her like she wanted. He left me the whole nasty speech that he wanted me to deliver at the end of the trip. Stuff so hurtful and vicious, Teddi would never send him another hyperspace postcard again. Stuff, I realized, I could never say to her. Anyway, I wasn't going to say them. I decided. I wasn't going back to the scanner.

I wasn't going back at all.

I squeezed her slender, tan hand. "Look, let's just have fun this week. Okay? You and me. That's why I came you know. To have fun. With you."

Her smile blossomed again.

Umph.

Every day we spent together, I saw more of her lovely smile. The resistance in her pale eyes dissolved. The resistance in her sun mellowed, slender body dissolved, too. She forgot about William. I felt that in her. For seven glorious days we explored the island and for six glorious nights we explored each other.

On the last day, sitting on the beach outside her bungalow, my toes jammed into the white, hot sand, I watched her dimpled, tanned ass as she waded in the surf and thought about how to tell her that I was staying. I was sure she would be glad. I was sure she would put me up and I'd be safe there. The port authority only had my hotel room address. I hadn't stayed there a single night.

I wasn't going back to New York ever. I would stay here with Teddi. I could teach wind surfing or something. I would be the William she wanted, the Will I wanted to be. William could go on being a body climbing, business monkey.

Teddi came up the beach then, lean and brown, her empty wine glass hanging from her fingertips. She stopped in front of me, legs splayed in the sand, salt water still trickling down her thighs. She's such a slim girl that a couple of glasses got her pretty tipsy. She told me, "I know he doesn't love me. I know he thinks I'm a brainless ass. I just wanted him to see all this. I thought that maybe if he did he would get it. He would want it. You know?"

"I know."

"But he'll never want it. He'll never change, will he?"

"No."

"But you get it. Don't you?"

I smiled.

"You want it, too. Don't you?"

I smiled again.

She did, too. "I'm glad." She threw the glass away. "Fuck him." Then she sank onto my lap, long legs wrapping around me. "You came. You've been sweet. Sweeter than he ever was."

I thought I would tell her then, but she smelled so damned good and she had the look in her eyes. "Come on ...." was all she said.

After would be soon enough ....

Sun pierced my eyelids, brighter than I remembered it being other days. Perhaps almost as bright as the first day I arrived here, except without the tear blurring pain. I opened my eyes.

The sea breeze lifted the sheers on the opened glass doors to Teddi's terrace. The tide had gone out over night, so the ocean pulled back from the beach exposing the sand bar there. I never felt so peaceful. I stretched under her cool cotton covers and sighed. Serene salt air filled my lungs.

The soft scrape of a door opening make me look toward the bathroom.

Ted came out toweling her hair. She was pink from the shower, nude and wet. She noticed me. "You woke up finally."

"What time is it?"

"Ten o'clock. You want to stop for brunch before I take you back to the space port."

I rolled onto my side, smiling.

She stopped toweling her hair. "What?"

"What if I said I decided not to go back?"

She blinked.

"What if I said I was going to stay?"

"You can't, Will. Your visa expires at twelve noon."

"Then what? I turn into a pumpkin?"

"God, are you serious? No dupe ever did that."

"There's a first time for everything." In my moment of giddy anticipation, I didn't notice that she wasn't onboard with the idea. Apparently, I didn't notice a lot of things that I should have. "You could help me. I could stay here."

She shook her head. "The port authority will come looking for you when you don't report to the scanner."

"No one knows I'm here, Babe. The only address I left was at the hotel. I haven't been there all week."

"They'll call William. He'll tell them about us. They'll come here."

Damn. She was right. Then I noticed that she kept her distance.

She said, "You have to go back, Will. It's the law."

I sat up. "I thought you would want me to stay."

She swallowed. She looked scared. What could I have possibly done to scare her? I was everything she wanted him to be. She said so. "Ted?"

"God, Will. I mean. Do I have to say it?"

I blinked.

"You're not real."

"But...." I thought of the last week. We laughed. We made love. We shared secrets. "We had fun."

"Yeah. Sure." She stared at me uncertain.

"God. Teddi, I love you. I love you more than he did. I love you like he never did."

She cracked a jittery smile, "yeah, it was fun."

God. God. God. How stupid could I have been? "What was that little speech on the beach last night?"

She just shrugged her shoulder. She *shrugged*. Last week meant nothing to her. I meant nothing to her.

I rolled out of bed, ignoring her when she jumped back. What was she afraid of? I didn't want to hurt her. I didn't want anything from her. All I wanted was to get the hell out of there. I yanked up my pants and put on my shirt, then dug my shoes out from under the bed. Her scent – the smell of citrus was all over the covers. It made me sick now.

"What are you doing?" She cringed by the bathroom door.

"Leaving." I found my overnight bag under the bed and checked it to make sure all my stuff was in there.

"Are you going back to the space port?"

I didn't answer, but headed for the glass doors. I stopped and looked back at her, "Teddi, do me one favor. Don't call them until you have to. Better. Don't call them at all. Please."

She nodded a little, pale eyes wide.

As I passed the picture window of her living room, I caught her standing in a bathrobe at her wall tall. The emblem for the port authority appeared on the screen, the dispatcher appeared. Why couldn't she wait?

I took off running down the beach. They can't confiscate me until my visa expires. I had to get lost. Fast. I didn't know where I was going, but it sure as Hell wasn't back into the scanner. I'm not burying my soul alive in that walking coffin back in the city.

I'm never going back.

Q-BIT'S ARROW

I was afraid to open my eyes. I was afraid that it was Monday.

Monday for the third day in a row.

If it was, then I failed. I laid in bed for a few precious seconds longer begging God for the miracle of Tuesday while anxiety stuck to my waking thoughts like clumps of wet lint. My brain stumbled manically through every line of code I proofed and every checklist I ran for the lab work yesterday. I was pretty freaked. Even in the module, I couldn't calm down enough to get totally rational. Maybe I screwed things up worse. There was only one way to find out.

I took long breath, let it out and opened my eyes.

The numbers lit on my bunk wall flicked to zero six thirty-three. They glowed, lighting up my consciousness. Zero. Six. Three. Three. I pushed my face into my pillow, gritting my teeth, "God, Cleo, what did you do?"

I eyed the clock again.

It was same hour to the minute that I woke when Monday looped for the first time.

Groaning, I turned on my side to face the walltall view from one of the few thousand cams that floated along the spokes of Jupiter-Jacco Station. Jove's belly bulged into the empty spacescape from above filling up the entire display. Oppressive and thick, it seemed to squash my tiny cabin. It looked identical to the view I saw at the start of the Monday loop. The ad for Carbostix floated down then the Carbostix Man started dancing and singing.

My gut sank.

Same as yesterday. Not definitive, I told myself, clinging to one last, comforting shred of denial. It could just be the morning programming slot for that particular commercial. I eyed Jupiter. No help there. Storms last hundreds of years and always look the same to me day to day anyway. I think the only people on the J and J who can tell the difference are the weatherheads in Meteorology.

Still, I had a feeling, but not a good one.

Slapping the release button on side of my bunk, my covers retracted.

As I sat up a nasty feeling of anxiety crept into my chest. My little cabin felt just as airless and coffin-like as it did the first few months after I arrived here. Swallowing the panic, I got up, stepped to my lav, ejected a couple of wipes and washed up. Routine settled me, so I brushed out my hair, braided it, scuzz-buzzed my teeth, then popped my locker, reached for a gray coverall and –

Stopped.

If this was Monday happening for a third time something in the quantum loop was going to change. I grabbed the navy blue coverall with big white lettering 'Jupiter-Jacco' that ran vertically down the right side of the torso, hip and pant leg. Sticking my feet in a pair of gravipeds, I headed for the Physics ring. Like yestermonday, I skipped breakfast in the commissary. Only this time it wasn't out of excitement for the success of the experiment, it was because of an awful gut sucking anxiety that I might not be able to break the Q-loop. If Monday was still hiccupping, I would know the moment I stepped through the threshold.

Bad News.

The Q-loop was still running.

When I got there, Sam and Yuki were bent over the spectrometer like yestermonday. From the door I could see where the light bands started checkering on the walltall next to them. Pure quantum activity. It was a huge disturbance like a ten on the Richter scale and they knew it.

Hearing me step in, they looked over their shoulders, eyes wide. "Man," said Yuki, "What are you doing in your module, Cleo?"

"Just tracking anomalies," I lied. "Why?"

They looked at the data on the walltall. Of course, the freezes for this morning's banding was completely skewed, casting a shadowy, quaking checkerboard pattern none of us ever saw before except in the simulator. This time though it was the real thing; a glimpse of the hiccup I created.

"There's a secondary pattern." Yuki said, "It looks like a time line divergence."

Actually, it wasn't like one, it was one. I was the only one aware of it though because I initiated it. "Theoretically, but obviously nothing has changed."

"That we know of...." Sam trailed as he looked at Yuki who looked at me.

For them living outside the Q-loop yesterday was Sunday and tomorrow would be Tuesday. There was no way I could explain what was really happening. My reality and their reality were intersecting, not concurrent. I pretended innocence and shrugged. "It's just data, guys. If we shifted time frames, don't you think we would know it?"

They looked at each other. Sam's brow crinkled.

Without waiting for an answer, I pushed open the door of my module and stepped in. Like the first trip through the quantum loop, the alternity horizon passed through me as I crossed the threshold. It was a faint, almost crackling pressure. After shaking off a moment of disorientation, I locked myself in and settled into my seat at the console. Touch pads glowing blue I looked across the room to the walltall, thumbed the screen pad and watched the streams of Q-bits begin to fill the panel like sand filling the belly of an hour glass. As the visuals for the running program piled up on the walltall, I pulled down the skullcap of the jelink, settling it on my head. After a tingle, we interfaced. The streams lifted into midair assuming their true interdimensionality. Sections of coded light frequency glided through the coordinates I vectored, appearing from the ceiling as they scrolled and then disappearing into the floor in the perpetual loop frame I created. That was what my Monday program looked like to the module processors.

I had the entire loop on file, so I could shut Monday off any time, but I was going for the gold here. I wanted to repeat the control, manipulate it and change the parameters. So far, all I could do was make Monday hiccup. I succeeded at that once. Last night I tried to save the file, but shut off the loop. Something went wrong and a third Monday popped up. The loop didn't terminate.

Frowning, I spread my fingers over the touch pads to begin re-sequencing the loop when a com pinged through the module. I winced, already anticipating the same conversation I had before. Twice.

"Cleo, you there?"

"I'm ass deep in work, Melody. What do you want?"

"How did things go Saturday night? Did you see him?"

Maybe the loop has some sort of inherent behavior parameter, but I caught myself saying, "Who?" even though I already knew the answer.

"The nipple biter."

"Melody." I groaned more irked with her habit for gross gossip this time than I had been the last two passes through the same comlink.

"Did you?"

I told her, "Hell, no. Not after you told me what he did to you. I blew him off. I went to the stims instead." I keyed up the red sequencer grid, watching it rise into my vision to intersect the waterfall of phasing code. "Now get off the com. I've got work to do."

I stayed in there the rest of the day hunched over my consoles and screens, head wedged in the jelink, trying to back track the code to find my mistake. After hours of fumbling with program patches, then hours more of trying to rewrite the tangled up mess I created, I was no closer figuring out how to tell the program to shut down. I would wake up tomorrow and it would still be Monday. It occurred to me that the loop I wrote was a fixed circular segment in time. Maybe its very nature prevented me from changing it now. The hair on my arms stood up.

Brain sick and feeling like I was going to puke from being engaged to the system too long, I stared into those Q-bit streams whizzing through the module. I didn't want to loose this loop. It was my chance at fame and glory. I would be up there with Einstein. I would be beyond him. Way beyond. I would be the girl genius who programmed the first alternate reality vector.

The streams ticked along stubbornly through the blue glow of my module.

Gritting my teeth, I growled at them. The brutal truth was, I couldn't prove what I created here. I had no witnesses. The greatest scientific discovery in history didn't matter if I couldn't show somebody else what I did. Or could I? Sam and Yuki.

Giggling, I tapped my com. "Hey, Guys, I think I can clear up that secondary pattern anomaly you caught on the freezes."

The com crackled on a dead frequency. It made the little hairs on my arms stand up. I thumbed the hail pad again. "Hey. You guys."

Dead crackle.

Looking over my shoulder at the door of my module, I realized that they couldn't hear me. Just as they were locked out of the loop, I was locked inside it. Anything I did that violated the vector's loop parameters simply didn't phase with the rest of the preset shifting quanta. It nulled. Instantly. Sam and Yuki could never step into this module while this vector was running. Even if I stepped out and tried to lead them in, they would stay on their side of the mobius and I would end up in here. Maybe, something worse would happen. Who knows what would happen to a human being if they were forced to step out of their natural quantum sequence. Maybe nothing. Maybe death. I certainly wasn't going to risk it. They had to be in here with me as part of the operating locus when I jacked the power and engaged the code that would splice time-space and loop my slice of reality.

Those numbers kept cycling through my module like bees in a perfect, bright blue swarm.

God knows I'll never be able to take credit for the loop the way it's working now. All that was left to do was let it go. Flush the program. Get time back to normal. I did it once. Right? I'll do it again. Next time, I'll bring Sam and Yuki into the module with me.

For the moment I just wanted to make sure I could flush it.

I settled back into my chair, summoned the file and began deleting the frequency sequences. The coordinates fell away. The file shattered over the grid like blue embers showering a red hot grill, then they dissolved.

I looked at the walltall. The hazy, second checkerboard disturbance melted away. The loop began to collapse at last. Monday would stop hiccupping.

The deed done, I watched my precious discovery drain away into the wall tall.

Still feeling shaky and sick, I powered down the lab. Once the quantum processor unit is rebooted, the streams would reset to space-time normal. The alternity vector I created would stop vibrating. Reality would settle back into benign, static linear time.

The power down checklist finished, I closed my eyes and shut the last of the module down. The QPU went dark. The wall tall went dark. Finally, I lifted the skull cap of the jelink. My scalp felt like it was alive with worms from being linked so long. I sat there for minutes with nothing more than the touch pad lighting from console and shreds of lost genius floating in the air like smoke around my head. It was over.

What was the line from that Brando movie? In the blue dark I muttered, "I could a been a contenda."

So close to glory, but in the end I was no different than all the other module jocks in the department. Maybe it was a girl thing, but I felt like crying.

I pulled off the skullcap of the jelink. The window outside the door to my module was dark. If Sam and Yuki were gone, it must have been late and I hadn't eaten all day.

I felt more like a drink anyway. The Rats' Cellar wasn't too far, so I finished this miserable Monday the same way it started three days ago.

Like the other Mondays Jack Forster hunched over a suds less beer at one of the tables. He was a lowly dish jockey - worked on the array, so he didn't have much in common much of the weatherheads, the exogeologists, the engineers or any of the other departments on the J and J. They were brainware. He was just hardware from system operations. You can count the number of people in the Station Sysops department on one hand. They're glorified janitors. With an army of maintenance drones scuttling all over the array welding and splicing and what not, there isn't a lot of need for human maintenance workers, so who knows what Jack really does all day.

He was also Melody's 'nipple biter'. They went out a few times before they ended up in her cabin one night last week. I can't blame her. He was cute; still had some lean earth side muscle, not the slightly puffy-slack baby fat look that canned gravity gives people after a while no matter how much they work out in the gyms. If it wasn't for the nipple-chewing thing, I would have thought he was a nice guy. It was just bad luck that Melody was the first one on the station to find out that he was a freak in bed.

Being a newbie, only four weeks on the station, Jack wasn't starting off his tour on good terms with the female population. He couldn't buy a lay on the J and J now. In a can this small everybody watches out for each other. Word gets around fast, so stuff like obnoxious little sex habits spread like wildfire.

In spite of all that, I still felt a little sorry for the guy. Well, he brought it on himself. He's a pervert.

I zagged left to walk behind him hoping he wouldn't see me this time around. I made it all the way to the bar, ordered a beer and a plate of chicken fingers before. ...

"Hey, Cleo."

I pretended I didn't hear my name.

"Cleo," came from close behind then Jack touched my shoulder.

I winced at the sensation. It wasn't so much that the perv put his hand on me as it was a change in the vector. He didn't touch me during the last two trips, but then I didn't try to sneak by him either. It felt strange. For a second, I flashed on that feeling of walking through the alternity horizon in the threshold of my module. The same crackling wave of pressure pushed through me. The room started to tilt. Ignoring it, I turned toward Forster with a total lie of a smile on my face. "Hey, Jack."

"Where were you Saturday night?" was all I heard before it all spiraled away from me. The bar music, the voices, some girl's obnoxious squeal of a laugh all dopplered away. Jack's face whirled away down a white drain and I went with it.

Swimming up from anxious oblivion, I stretched under the cover, looking at the red of my eyelids. The past couple of trips through Monday drifted through my head, leaving me blandly anxious. Lying there, I walked myself through the lab work. The moment I ramped down the power input from the array and deleted the file the checkering on the walltall dissolved into space normal bands. The normal background static of competing threads returned. The loop was over. At least, it should be. Of course, it was. I took a deep breath and opened my eyes.

Thank God. The clock on my bunk wall read zero five-forty. I rolled.

The walltall showed blank space, not Jupiter's fat yellow-red-orange swirling gut. No Carbostix man either. No commercials at all. I tapped the release on my retainer cover and swung my legs out of bed. That's when I noticed something wrong. Really wrong. My legs were hairy as hell. They were a guy's legs. Guy's legs. Guy's arms. Guy's – everything. One quick, freaked out look around and I realized that this wasn't my cabin at all. The pictures of my sister and parents weren't tucked into the sides of the mirror over the lav. My Earth posters were gone. Nothing was the same. In fact, there was nothing in the cabin. No nick knacks. No mementos. Nothing. It looked like a newbie's cabin. Movement on the walltall across the cabin caught my eye. The display of empty space reflected like a dull, black mirror. A guy with sleepy, brown eyes and a bad case of bed head looked at back at me – at himself sitting on the edge of the bunk. It was Jack the Nipple Biter in his T-shirt and boxers. God! This was Jack's cabin. I didn't have a clue how, but the QPU must have looped me into his body. But. I shut down the experiment. I completely deleted the Monday vector. The Q shift vanished. Everything should be normal.

Even if it hadn't shut down, how could this happen?

I remembered the Rat's Cellar and the tingle when Jack touched my shoulder. Something happened to the vector when he touched me.

I looked at the body I was in. It gave me that feeling like when you see yourself on a walltall. You know how if you look at it long enough, you start to feel like you're not really there, like you're floating, like you're disconnecting from your body. I felt that. I was that.

The whole cabin started to fog over, so Jack stuck his head between his knees until it passed. That's when I realized that I wasn't in control. I was just floating along, snagged on his consciousness like a balloon.

As those black wads of cotton passed over, his head cleared some, so did I. Maybe deleting the experiment after initiating the Q-loop was impossible. Maybe the nature of the program itself negated deletion. On a circular time line, initiation would perpetually over ride the deletion and reset the program. So my deletion phase of the time line had no lasting effect. The Q-loop would continue to reset because initiation was always at the locus of the event. God. I could live my entire life in this one Monday. That is, if I age inside a Q-loop. I could be here forever.

But. It had to be more than that. It made some sense that the processor might keep rethreading my day, the coordinates matched, but how could it Q-loop my consciousness into another body? There had to be some anomaly in the thread. Infinite alternities. Maybe consciousness had vectors like time and space. I must have missed something. I must have made some tiny code change that sent the QPU spinning off on another vector on the grid. I had to get back to the lab, but how? Nobody was going to let a hardware head into the Physics labs for God's sake.

Groaning, Jack slipped out of bed. At his locker, he peeled out of his T. Sheesh, Jack. Nice abs. He pulled off his boxers. Sheesh, Jack nice... nice.

Then I noticed it. There was a wide, maroon crescent shaped bruise over his left nipple. There was actually broken skin. Jack never bit Melody.

She bit him.

Sheesh, Melody, what are you? A friggin' vampire? Now you're running around trashing the goofy newbie.

Though the teeth marks were scabbed over, they were angry, red and puckered, maybe infected. Jack touched it. We both winced. He should have gone to the infirmary, but I can't say I blame him for avoiding it. Talk about embarrassing.

He pulled on blue J and J coveralls, then made a face and squeezed himself. He had to 'go'. Even I could feel a pinch of urgency or maybe it was just one of those universal morning reflexes.

Jack stepped down the hall into an empty unilav, zipped down and drained himself. The guy pisses like a horse in the morning. Watching pee ping against the vacuum bowl, contentment washed up into my consciousness as his bladder emptied. It made me laugh. Human nature, you know. Then Jack chuckled, too. For a second, I thought he could sense me there with him.

As much as I needed to return to my module so I could figure out what was happening, there was no way of forcing Jack to go there and he hankered for eggs, so we headed for the commissary.

On the way, we passed Melody in the main habitat ring corridor. She started to smile as she came toward us with a cup of coffee and a banana-foil bundled in her dainty, little hands. Springy, blonde curls and springy, blonde boobs bouncing in time to her stride, she smirked and batted her lashes at us. "Hi, Jack," she sang in a phony coy voice. I wanted to slap that smug, two-faced sister silly.

Jack was too nice. Though his bitten pec twinged, he smiled, "Hi Melody," and started to slow down in spite of a rush of embarrassment.

She gnashed her teeth at us and kept going. Her giggle clattered against the narrow walls of the hallway. It gave us another twinge. Humiliation this time.

Jack just put his head down and made for the commissary. His cheeks turned hot.

Fight back you dumb newbie! But he wouldn't. Jack wasn't that kind of guy. I could see that now. Even when a girl dissed him, he wouldn't take her down. It might have been a little masochistic, but at least he had some class. Jack was a gentleman.

On the way, the corridor to the commissary seemed to close in, shrinking like some kind of nightmarish carnival fun house and then there was the sound. The muffled din of voices ringing up from the commissary seemed to echo through the habitat ring forever. It made Jack's ears buzz. At first, I thought the Q-loop was skewing again, but as near panic poured through us, it occurred to me that I felt this way when I first arrived on the J and J almost two years ago. It was plain old claustrophobia. We call it the squirms on the J and J, but it wasn't mine. It was Jack's. He had the squirms and he had them bad.

His heart started pounding. He started to hyper-ventilate. Poor, dumb newbie. Sweat popped out on his brow. He started to tremble.

I tried to urge him toward the next unilav we found. There was one just outside the commissary entrance. He thought he was going to get sick. He pushed through the door with his hand over his mouth.

Ahmed from Array Control was just zipping up. He glanced over then he looked over again, "You okay, Forster?"

Jack nodded. If he opened his mouth he might have puked.

Ahmed shrugged his brows and walked out without sanitizing his hands. *Ugh. What a pig.*

Jack grabbed a cold wipe from the dispenser and pressed it to his face with both hands. It settled him down. His breathing steadied. His heart slowed. After, he looked at himself in the mirror a long time. I never saw a look like that on anybody's face. It was pure misery. He hates being here. He really hates it. I caught one of his thoughts.

Four weeks, only four fuckin' weeks and I already look like the gray skinned station geeks that have been here forever.

Somebody's got to show this guy where the tanning salon is.

He pulled another wipe and sucked the water out of it to ease his cotton mouth. With the wipe hanging out between his teeth, he leaned forward to look at himself, gripping the rim of the sink in both hands. He groaned a little and rocked, looking like one of a nutcases from an asylum.

What a fuckin' huge mistake. He thought about how he should've stayed home; Earthside. He blinked and swayed for a second. *Fuckin' gravity.* He touched something on his nape. It was a scopolamine patch. The poor newbie must get can spins on top of the squirms.

That smell! God. Whole place wreaks like a fuckin' locker room. No fuckin' windows! No outside. Nothing. Space sucks. This place sucks. The people suck. The girls ... !

He spun and punched the wipe dispenser so hard the plastic backing popped off the wall screws. It crashed and slid across the floor making a lot of noise.

In fresh silence Jack panted, hardly noticing the pain in his hand from that punch as he stared at the broken wipe dispenser. He turned to the mirror once more, yanked the wipe out of his mouth and pointed at himself. "Six months." It sounded like a promise. We all have that clause in our contract. He could opt out and go home. Looking in the mirror, he seemed to be telling both of us, "Just don't leave here tied down to a stretcher, raving like a lunatic. The brainware will laugh."

He's right. They would.

Shit. They already are.

Being a lowly hardware head from systems operations, he wasn't even on their radar.

Groaning at his pasty reflection, Jack crumbled the wipe and pitched it at the recycle chute. We went to breakfast.

After all that he could still eat. Has to be a guy thing.

He squeezed ketchup all over his rehydrated eggs. Now that I think of it, ketchup was the only thing that made them edible. He started shoveling.

"Hey, Forster." A tray clacked on the meal table even before the body plopped down on the bench next to him.

Jack looked over. "Hal."

Another array jockey. I only remembered Hal because he has carrot orange hair and his face is so covered with freckles that it makes his blue eyes look demonically bright.

"Did that girl from Saturday night ever show up?"

Hal grinned, leaning toward Jack like he was expecting the punch line to a good joke.

Jack just sighed and kept eating.

Hal giggled sadistically. "Man. What a loser. You can't even score some ugly brainware chick from Physics?"

Hey.

"She's not ugly."

Thank you, Jack.

"Just flaky and crazy like all the girls on this station."

That's not fair. I thought you were some kind of tit biting pervert.

Hal laughed, "'Got that fuckin' straight." He slapped Jack's shoulder and told him, "When you get done here, Ahmed says it's your turn to space walk the array today. The crabs found some shorting panels. Probably micro meteors busted through the shielding. Have fun."

For the first time since I Q-looped into his head, Jack looked forward to something. He might have hated the J and J. He might have hated the food, and the people, but he liked his job and he loved space walks.

Once the airlock lit green, the outer door irised as Jack shuffled forward and snagged the tow bar with his leash. He trembled, but it wasn't from fear it was from the rush. This was only cool thing about being on the J and J for Jack. We looked around. Jupiter was everywhere. There's no other way to put it. It throws this yellow glow on everything. It's totally surreal. He paused, taking it in. He loved it out here. He could sit out here for hours using up oxygen just staring at Jupiter if not for the scary buzz of background radiation in his earphones.

Even in his radiation suit, exposure was limited to an hour a week. No more. The crabs do most of the work outside. He floated out, double checked his tools and told the bar through his mike, "Array Sector nine, six, nine," then started the exposure timer on his sleevetop as the bar pulled him into the array.

After a couple of connects, the tow bar slowed to a halt on the track, giving him some time to compensate for momentum with the little thruster on his suit. He gave the ignition button a couple of light touches, stalling expertly over the cluster. He was pretty good at working the thrust module. He could handle himself in space. Not everyone can.

Jack, you're impressing me.

Better than the first time I came out here and over burned. I almost tore the friggin' leash off my suit, Ahmed saw it from the monitors. He was still laughing his ass off when I stepped through the lock.

Maybe Jack could sense me. Maybe he thought I was just part of the internal dialogue that goes on in everybody's head all the time.

The cluster with the problem was covered with crabs. Their maintenance arms all stuck up like so many little mechanics throwing up their hands in frustration. Jack keyed the dismiss command on his sleevetop and they scuttled off the panel to let him approach it.

Next he keyed the access door. As it opened, he hooked his leash onto the rail inside and somersaulted in gracefully despite the thruster and the bulky spacesuit. He would be fun to bounce around with in the Zero-G bubble. He was agile as an acrobat.

According to his sunshield screen the problem was in the power relays. His exposure timer pinged, letting him know he had forty minutes left including the tow ride back to the lock. Not a lot of time, but he wasn't worried in the least. It struck me. Jack was good out here. He belonged out here. He shouldn't go back to Earth. The J and J needed him.

Luckily, he found the problem immediately. A short popped and spat sparks off the A-7 relay panel. Most of the wires were fried and melted.

Even insulated, the crabs couldn't get close without being shorted by a stray arc.

Easy fix, Jack thought.

He snapped the gator clips to the voltage meter watched it spike on one side, then clipped the other side. He smirked. Dead. Someone on the station was getting some nasty power surges. He keyed array coordinates into his sleevetop and watched the transformer codes roll up on his sunshield. Physics was the department getting zapped. My department.

Jack scoffed. *They're the biggest power hogs on the station anyway.* He keyed again, locking in the specific lab module being affected. Number sixty-nine rolled up on his shield.

"Cleo's module," he huffed, breath briefly condensing on the face plate of his helmet before the EVC circulator in there evaporated it. "Bitch."

I guess I deserved that. The truth was I didn't care what he called me for the moment. Jack found the vector anomaly. My anomaly. It was the surge. It had to be.

I hope her precious flux data got just as deep-fried as this panel. Serves her right.

Yeah, yeah. Just fix it for me, Jack.

According to the service order glowing on his sunshield display, the transformer started arcing this morning. Any of the surges could have easily garbled some of the code in the loop program I wrote. I was lucky the entire QPU grid wasn't fried.

So much for being Miss Brainiac. He snickered, enjoying my misery a little too much.

I could let it run a few more days, maybe a week and totally goose her research. She'll never catch it. The power consoles in her module can't read the surges on this end. She would think she was rerouting power like usual.

Jack. Don't.

He cackled in his helmet. *Let her dangle for a couple of days. Screw her.* Just as he was about to push off -

Jack. Please don't.

He stopped. He looked around.

Jack. You hear me? Fix it. Please, please, please fix it.

He looked at the panel again.

Please. Jack.

There is a service order. He eyed the panel. So, I would probably get caught delinquenting a repair. Fine with me. It would get me tossed off the Jupiter-Jacco sooner.

He started to push off again.

Jack!

He shirked and stopped. Shit. He looked at the panel again. He sighed. No sense in trashing my resume just to get back at a snobby, egghead bitch.

Okay. I'm a snobby, egghead bitch. Just fix it. Please.

Tripping the breaker switch, he popped the old panel, then floated down, slipped a replacement panel from the service compartment, slotted it, powered it up and gatored the two sides. Flow was back to normal. He closed up and glided up out of the relay pocket, catching his leash on the tow bar as he fed the burned panel to the crabs for recycling, then glided off into the Jupiterset like the Lunar Ranger.

"I'm so friggin' noble," he muttered, but his voice dopplered away with the rest of him.

In fact, the entire alternity began to flush the moment the relay was repaired. I went with it, whirling away from Jack, from Jupiter, from everything down that spinning white drain into nothing.

When I woke, the walltall across from my bunk scrolled an ad for the two-for-Tuesday night drink special at the Rat's Cellar on Jupiter's swirling belly. I was back in my own cabin, I was me again and Jack ....

Jack sat in his usual spot, alone at the end of one of the meal tables in the commissary, looking pale, homesick and hunched over his ketchup covered eggs.

He didn't look up as I stepped passed him on the way to the breakfast line. Why should he? Standing in line, picking up a tray, picking up my corn flakes and a can of milk, I kept looking over at him. The truth is everybody has a hard time adjusting to the J and J. It's not the easiest environment and it sure isn't natural. If you've got friends here, it's home and it's jammin'. It's the ultimate adventure. I guess if you don't have friends … it's just Hell in a spinning tin can.

The truth is, whether he knew it or not, that hardware monkey plucked me out of the Q-loop, so I set my tray on the table and sat down next to him.

I had no idea how our conversation ended last night, but whatever happened to me, I'm sure the whole thing played out the same for him. I blew him off. He looked annoyed that I came sniffing around again. I can't blame him. "Hey, Jack. Thanks for fixing the array yesterday. The surges were doing screwy things to my experiments."

He didn't bother looking at me, just shoveled away his nasty looking eggs and mumbled an obligatory, "you're welcome," around his mouthful.

"You want to try again. Going for drinks I mean."

He snorted sarcastically over his plate and gave his head a shake. "Don't think so."

"Why not?"

He shrugged and stuck another bite in his mouth.

"Give me one more chance. Come on," I nudged him. "The J and J isn't so bad. Lots of newbies get the squirms the first month or so. The can spins will disappear in another week or two."

He looked at me. Of course, how could I know he was phobic and dizzy?

His brown eyes cooled. He stabbed his eggs with his fork. "Who told you that? Melody?"

"Melody is an idiot."

His squint lost some of its angry tension. This was something we could agree on.

"I'll show you where the tanning salon is. You have to try out the Zero-G bubble. Have you been to the stims yet?"

He shrugged at his crappy breakfast. "I heard about them."

"I'll show you, okay? We'll go tonight."

"No. Thanks." He went back to shoveling away breakfast. He got so burned by the girls on this station, it was obvious he wasn't to going to waste any effort trying to connect again, not if he planned on leaving.

"You should give the J and J a chance. You're really good at your job. I know you like it. I know you like being out there with Jupiter over your shoulder, space walking the array. It's the ultimate. Don't opt-out."

He eyed at me again. "How did you know about that?"

I shrugged, pressed against his arm and beamed sincerity. "Come on. One more chance."

He looked me carefully. The tension in his face eased a little more. "Well."

"Jack," I pressed closer. "I promise. I won't bite."

Jack blinked, then hung his head and chuckled. When he looked at me again, his face was full of color and maybe a little anticipation. He asked me, "You ever been on a space walk?"

"Yeah, I have." I twinkled at him. "You ever been in a Q-loop?"

He crinkled his brow. "A what?"

I giggled, "Come on, I'll show you," grabbed his hand and pulled him out of his seat. "Jack, you are in for the ride of your life."

First published in *Quantum Muse*, March 2003.

A FRIEND IN NEED

Jonz gulped air at the top of the compartment then dove under, hands outstretched, clawing for the walls, the floor below, a door jam, any thing that would tell him where he was in his cabin. The electrical systems in the Fitzgerald must have shorted out when it began filling with water. It happened fast. In the few seconds that the impact bounced Jonz out of his sleeping sling, water began exploding through the ventilation ducts with the pressure of a fire hose, then the lights went out. The icy grip of roaring water closed around him in seconds.

Liquid dark pressed up against Jonz's eyes, inspiring a queer strength sucking panic. Blind and weightless in cold, alien water, disorientation numbed his mind and body instantly. He reckoned the impossibility of escaping if he couldn't find the door. The ship was probably already ten or twenty meters under water, maybe more. It wasn't even supposed to be submerged. It wasn't supposed to be planetside at all. The Fitzgerald was a space ship; a surveyor running map scans of the surface when Jonz went to bed just last night.

No alert ever sounded.

Fingers brushing something soft; the webbing of his sling, he grabbed it and gave it a hard tug. If he could figure out which wall it was attached to, he would know which direction to swim. His cabin door was opposite the sling wall. Jonz pulled it taut. By a small miracle, he happened to be pointed in the right direction, but he needed air again. Triangulating off the sling, he pushed off the floor and found his air pocket once more.

It was much smaller. Only his face fit in the surface of the pocket. Dark there, too. The only way Jonz knew he had surfaced was by the cold seam that rung his head, along the edges of his hair line, cheeks and chin. He took several breaths, hyperventilating, using up the last of the O-2. He was going to have to try to make the long swim out. If there was a way out.

Puffing, half panicking, he knew he wasn't going to make it. There would more pitch black corridors and airlocks to negotiate. A few rational thoughts flaked off, mercifully spoiling his terror. Maybe the way the ship was flooding, there was a big hole some where. There had to be a big hole. Maybe he would get lucky and see it right away. If there was light. If it was day. He took his last breath and dove, pushing off the ceiling as he plunged for the door. He found the catch quickly, twisted it and pulled the door open. Weighted by the turbulence of the filling cabin, it resisted until he fumbled for the jam, managed to anchor himself with one hand and draw it open with the other. He found the other jam and pushed off with such force that he hit the opposite wall face first. He recoiled, nose blossoming with pain and released several fat-precious bubbles of air.

The corridor was another black wall of roaring nothing, but he was still oriented with his back to his cabin, so he reached out and found one of the zero-g rails. He turned toward the bow and began hand-over-handing, his own hands no more than faint smudges darting through thick, icy-black wool. Calmed by progress, encouraged by momentum, he began to think that he might make it. The first emergency airlock wasn't that far from his cabin. Maybe seven or eight meters. No more.

The ship began to list. The wall tipped toward Jonz. He clamped tight to the invisible rail, terrified of losing contact with it in the absolute dark. The ship swayed, then shuddered hard, beating him against the wall. Jonz lost more bubbles.

This time he glimpsed them. Giggling silver slivers wriggled passed his head up into the darkness. Straight up. His motion starved eyes followed them. Far above, he saw the faint golden shimmer of the surface burst through the orafice of the fractured hull. The entire bow section of the Fitz' was gone.

Jonz climbed like Hell, eyes on that blessed, murky golden dawn as it slowly filled the end of the corridor. The weight of the propulsion units aft must have been tipping the ship vertical. That meant Jonz had only seconds to get out. Once the Fitz' was perpendicular with the bottom, it would plunge straight down. Anything in its slipstream would be sucked down with it.

Jonz burst out of the hole like a missile, launching himself off the ragged steel of the hull hard with his bare feet, careless of whether they got cut or not. For seconds, momentum pushed him toward the surface, toward air that he hoped he could breathe. He glided up, letting his oxygen starved, aching thighs rest, letting the ballast of air in his lungs lift him toward golden salvation. As he rose, a shadow melted into focus on the surface. There was something in the waves.

A life raft? Did others make it out, too?

He kicked for the surface, hoping Ames, or Michelle was in that boat. Any of the crew would do. The only thing worse than dying on some barren, alien world would have been being the sole survivor on a barren, alien world. They might have rescued the emergency transmitter. Maybe rations, too.

Jonz kept kicking, but neither the shadow nor the surface were getting closer. Lungs beginning to burn, he kicked harder. The current shifted around him. The slipstream consumed the water column around him. Like great cold coils, it closed around his aching muscles and pulled him down. The Fitz got him and was dragging him down with it. He fought it, clawing strokes, kicking madly while his strength drained away and muscles began to burn, then cramped into knots of paralysis. Dark blotches passed over his vision. His lungs cramped and knotted. His heart pounded as he flailed, but made no progress.

The golden promise of air above remained out of reach. In those last seconds, lungs raging for air, trying to trick Jonz into inhaling water, he looked up at the shadow on the surface and knew he wasn't going to make it. Vision vibrating to the agonized beat of his heart, he refused to breathe, but his mouth opened regardless of his will. Water rushed in. As it filled his mouth, cold enough to hurt his teeth, he kept looking up. Vision filling with dark wads of cotton, he thought he saw the shadow on the surface suddenly elongate and dive toward him.

The soft mew of gulls brought Jonz around. He stirred with a smile, realizing he must have dozed off on the beach. Race Point was peaceful this early in the season. No tourists cluttered up the beach. There was just the soft breath of the Atlantic and the June sun.

Sudden pain rolled him on his side. Jonz came around wetly hacking, cheek in the orange talc of a beach that was light years away from Cape Cod. By the time he finished sputtering and spitting, he remembered the Fitz', the water and, most of all, drowning. His water logged chest stung as he rolled onto his back.

The sky was muddy. The sun in this solar system hid coyly behind ruddy veils of iron dust and water vapor clouds. It reminded him of Mars, but with a more temperate climate and habitable levels of O-2. The bloody flavor of the air here lingered in Jonz's mouth as he sat up. Spitting did nothing to relieve him of the taste.

He found himself in the same T-shirt and boxers he went to bed in. They were dry, though caked with the russet colored sand of the beach. His thighs got scraped up; nicked and bleeding a bit. He inspected the dozens little punctures in his legs. They were deep. Shaky and feverish, he couldn't remember how they happened, but wondered vaguely about infection.

Around him, he noticed pieces of the Fitz' washed up on the receding tide. Other than the debris from the ship, the was no sign of his crew mates. Except, someone else must have survived. Somebody pulled him out of the water.

The gulls mewed.

Gulls?

Jonz looked into the sky. Sea gulls on this planet?

Then he felt the presence; the absolute sensation of surely and certainly being watched by something his mammalian brain could not possibly reckon. The feeling of Otherness that bore down on his tiny human proportions, penetrated his awareness on a cellular level. All the hairs on Jonz's body prickled erect. The terror he felt out in the water was nothing compared to the stuff that trickled through his brain like ice water as he turned his head slowly.

Just a few steps away, the thing crouched on a long shelf of rock behind Jonz. He stared at it a long time over his shoulder. His shock stalled by a moment of curious bewilderment. He couldn't decide whether the thing was organic or mechanical or some weird amalgamation of the two. It resembled a giant, three ended slinky covered with loose, gray elephant's hide. It hunkered on two of its thick-baggy coiled stalks. At the top of the arch that joined its fat-springy legs, the third gray, baggy stalk poised in the air, curled into a tapered question mark. A whorl of thick spiny bristles festooned the blunted end.

The pattern on the creature's muzzle matched the pattern of punctures on Jonz's legs. He wondered if the thing attacked him out in the water. Maybe those bristles were poisonous. Maybe he was dinner. He didn't move, just stared at it.

After a moment, a tiny aperture opened in the center of the bristles. "Eeee-youu." It said, then, "Jonzzzz." Its stalk lolled to the left. It said in its high gull voice, "Do not be afraid," then lolled to the right. "I am tasting your language."

"Tasting -- you mean you can communicate with me?"

"Comm-Eeeeuuunicate. Yes. Better and better, Jonz. I taste your fear. Don't be afraid. I don't eat you. You're safe."

Jonz noticed his sore legs. "You pulled me out of the water."

"I pulled you out."

He rolled over onto his knees, moving slowly partly out of caution, partly out of weakness. "Thank you."

The mass of fat walrus bristles wriggled.

Jonz looked down the beach, then up into the orange dunes. If it saved him, maybe --

"I pulled no others out of the water, Jonz."

He squinted at the creature. Apparently it could taste his thoughts, too. He looked along the tide line. A long way down the beach, other things began to wash up. He noticed a crate in the shallows. Almost anything from the ship would be useful. He noticed the creature. It seemed content to squat on the out cropping. It told him in plain English that he was safe. He had no alternative but to believe it was sincere as well as intelligent, so he started cautiously away from it, heading up the beach to check out the crate. He glanced back a few times, but the creature remained on its rock.

When he reached the crate, he glanced back once more.

The creature swayed back and forth on its heavy, saggy trunks. Its bristled stalk craned in the air.

Jonz sloshed into the surf. The crate turned out to be food stuffs from the mess hold. Cases of instant potatoes. It might as well have been manna from Heaven. He grabbed the handle and gave it a tug, but the tide jammed it into the orange silt, so he knelt in the water to start digging the thing out with his bare hands. Lungs hypertensive from inhaling the alien sea water, the exertion brought on a near convulsive and very painful coughing fit.

Jonz staggered back in the wash, hacking wetly until his chest cramped. If that wasn't bad enough, the commotion brought the creature running … sort of. Out of the corner of his eye, Jonz spotted it launch itself from the out cropping. To his horror, it came end over ending just like a giant, enraged slinky. In spite of its girth, its big, round peds made a soft mmmf-mmmf sound as it came up the beach at him.

Still gurgling and wheezing, Jonz scrambled from the surf to get out of the way of the creature as it mmmf-mmfed along the sand, stirring up clouds of orange talc. It slinkied pretty damned fast.

It made a straight line for the crate.

Helpless to defend his only food, Jonz stumbled up the sand and fell there, weak and chest cramping from the coughing fit. He watched the creature as it slinkied into the wash. It squatted in the water, wrapped its long stalk around the box and began rocking it loose. At last, it pulled the crate free, then rolled it out of the tide up onto the beach.

Dizzy, Jonz wheezed. Now his legs were rubbery. Vague knotting pain settled in his joints. He wondered if he could have the bends or something worse. This was an alien world. He could have inhaled any thing out there in the water or in the air for that matter. He felt like puking. He let his head fall back on the sand and closed his eyes.

Mmmf-mmmf. Mmmf-mmmf.

Though a panic reflex urged him to get to his feet, Jonz didn't twitch a muscle. A fresh blush of fever burned the strength out of him.

"Jonzzz."

He opened his eyes, swallowing an unpleasant urge. The creature blocked out the muddy sky. Gently, it set the crate down beside him and said, "You are very sick from the water."

Lying at its tree trunk sized feet, Jonz wasn't inclined to respond. The orange world dipped and rolled like the Fitz' did just before it went down. Unholy nausea rolled around in his belly solid and heavy as a bowling ball. The first lurch caught him by surprise. He rolled onto his hand and knees just in time for the second.

As that bowling ball inched up his esophagus with each fresh heave, the creature said very softly, "You'll be all right," as it wrapped the end of its trunk around his brow, "I'll take care of you."

It held his head while he finished throwing up.

"Jonzy, are you sure you are strong enough to go down to the beach today?"

"Yes, Gull. Stop worrying." Jonz said, knocking orange dust off his boots. Gull, that's what he named the creature, shuffled closer, extended its trunk so that its bristles momentarily tickled his cheek.

"Yes. Your fever is down and you feel well, but why do you have to go down to the beach? I brought many boxes of food from the ship. You should rest more."

Jonz noticed the stacks of crates resting against the cave wall. While he recuperated, Gull made several dives on the Fitzgerald to retrieve food, clothing, even the navigator's console chair so that Jonz had some where other than rocks and sand to sleep on. He had never seen Gull swim … except for the first time when it saved him, but watched it enough over the passed week to realize that its coiled skeleton and musculature were incredibly dynamic. It could flatten, twist and elongate itself into almost any shape. It was remarkably strong and, he discovered, a habitual doter. Of the later, Jonz couldn't complain. If Gull hadn't pulled him out of the water, resuscitated him, then took care of him for the passed seven days while he fought off whatever native microbe make him so damned sick, he would be as dead as the rest of his crew. He owed Gull his life. "You said that you brought up several boxes that weren't food, right?"

"I placed them in the cave by the inlet."

Jonz got to his feet and started from the cave. "Well, one of them might be the emergency transmitter."

Gull shuffled after him like a giant caterpillar, its bristled trunk hung over Jonz's shoulder. "You mean that others will come to find you?"

"Gull, we've got surveyors mapping out this entire sector. If I can find the transmitter and activate it, someone will hear it and coordinate a rescue."

They stepped out into dirty ochre light of morning.

"More humans," Gull cooed, "Jonzy, that would be wonderful."

Jonz chuckled, "You bet your ass it would be wonderful." He noticed the wreckage of Gull's ship against a distant hill side. Fractured, pitted and heavily weathered, russet dunes swallowed two thirds of the hull. There was no telling how long Gull had been stranded here. Intuition told Jonz that his gentle alien friend had been planet wrecked for a long time, maybe hundreds or even thousands of years. "When they come, we'll both get off this rock. Maybe we can send you home, too."

"Home. I have been here so long, Jonzy, this is home." Gull clucked. "But I am eager to meet more humans."

Jonz shrugged his brows. "Have it your way."

"Yes. Of course."

Jonz chuckled.

They made their way to the inlet cave.

The transmitter was there among the things that Gull pulled from the sunken ship. Jonz carried it up to the top of the cliff above the cave. Gull followed, protesting all the way, complaining that he was exerting himself too much, but Jonz ignored it and pushed on. He wanted as much elevation as possible so that the transmitter had a clear path with no geology to block the signal. A little winded, he puffed as he set the pivot anchors, the geomagnetic driver, mounted the dish, then said a little prayer and flipped the switch to the tiny breaker. The battery light flickered and lit. The red bar on the charging meter began to fill with a green column. When it peaked, the dish began to whir, moving into position to begin its transmitting routine.

"Thank God," Jonz said, so relieved to see the transmitter working that he didn't take much notice of the peculiar tingling in his toes.

"You're not well, Jonzy."

"I'm fine." He shirked off Gull's doting bristles and looked out over the ocean. Dirty slivers of light flickered across the brown waters. The bloody smelling wind keened across the cliff face. It was the first truly quiet moment Jonz experienced since the crash. He had been too ill since waking up on the beach to think of much else but survival. Now though, he thought of his crew mates down in the water, melting away in the red silt. Out of one-hundred and nineteen people on board, he couldn't believe he was the only one who made it out alive. He was just a data stream tech. He still had no idea what happened, why the ship came down. If he had the black box...

"Gull?"

"Yes, Jonzy?"

He swallowed a fresh wave of nausea. "Could you dive on the Fitz' one more time for me."

"Of course, Jonzy."

They went out the beach several days in a row together. It took Gull a few dives to locate the black box, dig it out and bring it to the surface. Each morning, Jonz watched his alien friend wade out into the surf. Gull elongated into a long, nearly flat ribbon of gray flesh, then undulated effortlessly over the yellow crests of the waves and disappeared without any splash beneath the wash. Jonz continued onto the sea cliff to maintenance the dish and see if any messages bounced in from another surveyor. Gull didn't like him making the climb to the transmitter.

Somehow, it sensed that he wasn't well. He hadn't said anything, but his fever seemed to come and go, and the tingling in his feet grew intense in the evenings. Even worse, most of the puncture wounds on his thighs, though they had scabbed over, were swollen and red mottled. He couldn't bear to tell Gull that the cuts were infected. He had a feeling that it would have felt guilty.

Stretched out in the navigator's console, Jonz played the disc from the flight recorder over and over until Gull took it away from him. "It's not good for you to listen to them."

It was right, of course. Although the sound of human voices was a comfort, it was also the terror riven sound of his crew mates and his friends dying.

Jonz shook his head. The best he could figure from the bridge audio was that the ship had been pelted by micro-meteors. Crippled, they decided to try to make a landing on the planet. It was no wonder the alert never sounded. A lot of systems failed almost instantly by the sounds of the bridge crew. They had planned a landing once they finished the preliminary mapping and scanning. Apparently, they managed to belly into the atmosphere and glide in. They almost made it, tried to ditch, but must have hit the water at to steep an angle and broke up.

Jonz knew how they died. Most of them died when the ship struck the water, but a lot of the men and women in the crew's quarters aft probably survived the ditch like him. They must have drowned. It was terrifying down there in the cold, in the darkness. It was terrifying to take that last aching breath of icy water and know what was happening, to be utterly helpless, strangling alone and light years from home in an alien yellow sea.

Jonz noticed Gull shuffling around near the food stuffs, bristles flicking over the crates, maybe inventorying them. He huffed at his luck. He lived because the ship broke in half just a few meters in front of his cabin. He lived because Gull was there to pull his water logged carcass out of the sea. He lived because that thing took care of him, salvaging food and water from the sunken ship.

Jonz began to cry. He didn't know why. Maybe it was gratitude, or regret, or the unrelenting pain in his feet. Gull came at once and curled around him, rocking him, console and all in its giant baggy, gray folds until he fell asleep.

In the morning Jonz pulled back his covers. His legs were worse. The mottling turned into thick maroon bruises. Some of the wounds were raised and hard as walnuts. Still, he didn't feel too bad, so he eased out of his chair. His legs felt a little shaky at first, but they steadied under him.

Gull saw them and told him, "You shouldn't go to the transmitter today."

Jonz went anyway. He was damned glad he did.

The receiver captured a transmission over night.

Legs aching, fever sweat running down his brow, Jon sat down next to the transmitter, kissed it, and played the incoming message. "This is the

USS Kaslovsky. We copy your distress signal, USS Surveyor Fitzgerald, and are relaying your coordinates to the USS Surveyor Mifflin-Ulysses to alter course to your location and initiate recovery operation. ETA two solar weeks. Please acknowledge."

Giggling, Jonz flicked the mike switch, gave the Fitz' call and told the Kaslovsky, "Got your message loud and clear. Have supplies to hold me until you arrive. Can't wait to see the Mifflin-Ulysses drop into orbit. Over."

He punched the send pad. It would be a few hours before they received it, but they would know for certain that someone was alive and waiting for rescue.

Jonz told Gull, "They're coming."

"That is good, Jonzy. That is very, very good."

He nodded, giggling like a giddy little kid, then tried to get up. His thighs spasmed violently and he went down with a wail, clutching at the bone crushing cramps in his quadriceps.

Gull carried him back to the cave.

Jonz spent the rest of the day in the navigators' console watching the lumps on his thighs swell and pucker like grapefruits. His feet went numb. He began to perspire heavily and vomited until his stomach muscles cramped. He began to think that he wouldn't make it through the night, let alone two weeks until the rescue ship came.

Gull kept bringing him water from the ship stores. It was the only thing he could keep down. After darkness fell, the throbbing in his legs began to knock his consciousness back and forth like a frenetic ping-pong ball. He sensed himself slipping under, felt a faint pang of panic and tried to calm himself, tried move his mind away from the pain, away from those oddly distant, terrifying thoughts of death. In the dark, above him, the air twinkled like bubbles trapped against the cave ceiling. They glittered like stars. Then, staring at them long enough, Jonz began to think he was outside. He saw stars overhead. As he watched, he noticed one moving across the sky. Was it the rescue ship? He raised his arms and called to it.

Someone shook him.

The touch sling shotted Jonz back into the center of the muscle shearing pain in his legs. He howled.

Gull was there, stuffing something in his mouth.

He choked and fought for a second.

"Pain killers," it said frantically.

Jonz gulped down all he could. Not long after, he grew fuzzy and comfortable. Sleep crept over the top of him for a few merciful hours before dawn.

Light against his lids brought Jonz fluttering to consciousness. Pretty ochre beams of light shown through the mouth of the cave. The red dust whirled and cavorted in them like the happy specters of his dead crew mates. He stared at them a while, gratefully mindless and painless.

Then he realized that he was numb from the waist down. Jonz pushed back his covers. His thighs were a mass of bloated yellow nodules. From his knees down, his legs were black and withered. He screamed, "Gull!"

It came to his side at once. "It's all right, Jonzy."

"Do something!" Too weak to shout again, he rasped, "my legs!"

"Yes, it's splendid, isn't it?"

"What?" He looked at his legs again. Thick shadows squirmed in some of the nodules. "God! What are they!"

"My children, Jonzy."

"God! What did you do to me!"

"Jonzy, don't be upset. Look how fat and vigorous they are. I've never seen them pupate so quickly." Gull began to shuffle away. "It's that iron rich blood of yours. Oh, splendid. Thank you, Jonzy. Thank you. I will make sure that the children always taste your gracious sacrifice."

"Gull!" A queer tickle in his thighes made Jonz look down at them.

The first one erupted, chewing through Jonz' skin, bristles first, then wriggled out until It rolled out of its bloody cocoon to plop onto the sand. It slinkied quickly out of reach, crying, "Eee-yoou, eee-youuu."

Jonz screamed and wrenched around, trying to escape the dead, heaving-wriggling half of his body.

Inspired by the cries of their siblings, all the others began biting through his skin. Hatching out in twos and threes, they dropped to the cave floor and slinkied quickly away, their mews chorusing.

Gull paused at the mouth of the cave, "Now there are more humans coming. My family will grow quickly."

"Gull..." Jonz uttered, too weak to draw the blanket over his bloody, dead, black-shrunken legs.

"I'll maintenance the transmitter today. I don't want the others to lose their way. You make such fine mothers. Oh thank you, Jonzy. Thank you."

Published in: *Beyond the Borderline Science Fiction Webzine*, May/June 2001; *Aphelion Science Fiction Webzine*, October 2001; *Alternate Realities Science Fiction Webzine*, November 2001.

LIFE BOAT

Jon Gordon shrugged deeper into his seat in front of the camera. In spite of the shadowy hollows around his eyes, his pallor and the obvious signs of malnourishment, he smiled and seemed quite relaxed. "First things first," he said, "I'm didn't agree to do this interview get my name in the papers. I think there's been enough publicity about the crash and I'm certainly no hero, just a survivor. I just want to clear Captain Jackson's name. I just want people to know that he did his best to bring us all home."

He glanced off camera, dark eyes flashing like beads, distracted by something, perhaps started. After six weeks cooped up in a tin can shaped like a ten meter cigarette with nothing but attitude thrusters and the crackle of a damaged radio, it wasn't surprising that he went a little mad.

He glanced off camera again, smiled and said, "Oh, yes. When the micro meteors hit the Columbe, decompression alarms sounded all over the ship. We had only seconds to get to the pods. I made it to the aft life boat along with Mai Chung and Danny Webster." He paused again, apparently listening to the next question. A strained smile flickered across his face, "When the boat jettisoned, we pretty much knew it was over for the surveyor. As we departed, we could see the Columbe through the portals. It just disintegrated. I saw one other boat out in the debris field after, but it looked dead in space. Thrusters never powered up."

He paused again, cocking his head then answered the silence, "Captain Jackson couldn't have prevented it. It was a freak accident." He fell quiet again, then squinted, dark eyes glinting manically, "For God's sake, we were flying through the Belt. Do you know how much debris is whizzing around out there? It amazing something like this hasn't happened before. It's a dangerous job. Everybody on the Colombe knew that or they wouldn't have signed on." He listened again, brows burrowing deeper over his eyes. Obviously, he didn't like the inferences that the interviewer attempted to draw out of him. He snapped, "Look, if all you want to do is hang Captain Jackson post mortem, you got the wrong guy. This interview is over." He started up from his seat, froze, eyed something off camera. The angry twinkling in his brown eyes faded. His face relaxed. "Okay. I won't leave. Yet." He said. He eased back into his seat. "What do you want to know?"

He listened for a minute or so, tugging at the sleeves of his filthy flight suit, apparently tidying his appearance for the benefit of the camera. At last, he answered. "How did I survive? I have to give Mai credit for that. And Danny. We knew right away that we were likely to be stuck in that damned pod for a while. We rationed the emergency stores. We gave ourselves a routine …. You know, something to keep us sane. We sang songs, played word games, talked about our families. We took shifts trying to fix the radio, watched space for a rescue ship. None came." His eyes grew wide for an instant. His mouth rippled oddly against a surge of hysteria. Then he was calm and collected again. His smile twitched relieving his expression of the slack mania that had softened all the muscles of his face over his many weeks folded into a sitting position in that tiny lifeboat with the rotting bodies of his companions.

His dark eyes glinted at the next question, "Well, Danny died first. He was a diabetic. He had a pump implant, but he was scheduled for a refit in sickbay the afternoon of the accident. Rotten luck, huh? He lost consciousness and slipped away from us. He was in the last seat." Jon nodded over his shoulder at the darkened space behind him as if he expected his friend's corpse to be there. He huffed, tears glimmering in his eyes "Really, he was the luckiest one. He just went to sleep and didn't wake up." Jon sniffled and smeared off tears, already nodding, "Yeah. We did. Once the rations were all gone. We had to." He looked into the camera suddenly, dark eyes lightless, wide and frightened. "It wasn't my idea. Mai did all the cutting. She figured out that we could cook the meat on the heat dissipaters if we pulled up the floor panels in front of her seat." He swallowed heavily. "But, there were parts we didn't eat. Couldn't eat. What was left of Danny started rotting. Mai put it all in the waste tubes and jettisoned it. She was the only one small enough to climb back and forth over the seats and through the fuselage."

He grew quiet a moment, expression becalmed as he looked at his thin hands gathered in his lap. He sighed softly, seemed to be reconciled, even peaceful. "Yes, she did. I woke for my shift and turned to talk to her. She was so still. Her eyes were closed. I thought she fell asleep listening to the radio. I was mad, then I looked down." His mouth stretched as he whimpered, "Mai cut herself. She cut her wrists." He hid his face in his hands and sobbed and rocked. "She left me alone in that damned thing. She left me alone. She left me. She left. She ...." He hiccupped and drooled and buried his face in his knees and rocked furiously for minutes while he wept.

Grief spent, he straightened in his cramped seat, snuffed and mumbled an apology for breaking down. He sat quiet a long time, head cocked, wet, swollen, empty gaze vaguely searching for some thing off to the left. In a tiny, weak voice, he said, "after that I was alone."

He glanced furtively over his shoulder as if he thought the seats behind him were occupied. His shoulder twitched spasmodically; a chill run amok through his frenetic conscience. Maybe he still heard his dead shipmates' voices in his head. The poor bastard.

He listened a moment, dark eyes narrowing again. "Why are you asking me about that?" He shook. "They were my friends. My shipmates. I didn't want to. I didn't have a choice. I just wanted to survive. For me. For them." Outrage wrenched the muscles in his face. You don't understand!" His eyes emptied, turned black and bottomless. "You can't understand!"

Then Jon Gordon grabbed the handle of the hatch and snapped, "This interview is over!" He jerked it hard. The airlock released and Jon launched himself out into space. He spun away, flailing as he ballooned inside his flight suit into the endless darkness.

I flicked the monitor off and turned in my seat.

Scored and pitted, the lifeboat rested beside me in the recovery bay of the salvager. All that was left inside it, other than Jon's last log, was Mai's half eaten, desiccated body, still strapped into her seat. The scant evidence of her suicide showed in the thin tears in her leathery wrists. Sandwiched between a dead man and a mad man in a narrow metal coffin, spinning endlessly through darkest reaches space with a dead radio, no rescue signal, no food or water left, she realized there was only one way out.

But Jon never gave up hope. Poor Jon.

He never gave up.

THE BULLIWOGS

Talmidge twisted my arm behind me with one hand, while he pushed my face toward the water with the other. "Drink it and I'll let you up."

Billy Booley stood behind us chanting, "Drink it. Drink it. Drink it."

Of course, I wouldn't. Any water on Shiners that hadn't been through the plant was too dangerous to touch, let alone drink. Anyway, it smelled bad. Really bad. Like skunk spray. As it was, I held my breath for a long as I could. The smell was so bad, just breathing it made me want to puke. Worse, little things twitched and swam around down in that thick, murky brown water.

Talmidge twisted my arm more, making my shoulder hurt worse. My elbow twinged painfully. "C'mon, Becky. One drink."

My breath burst . "Oooow! Talmidge, you're hurting me!"

"*Daaah.* One sip and I'll stop."

I caught a deep whiff of the swamp, almost gagged, and yelled at him, "Talmidge, stop it or I'll tell."

He just laughed and tried pushing my head into the water, but I pushed back, yelling, "Stop it!"

Just then, somewhere behind me Tommy Choi said, "Cut it out. It isn't funny."

All the sudden Talmidge let go of me. When I sat up, I saw Tommy had a fist full of Talmidge's T-shirt. He twisted around and they started punching each other. Being a little smaller, Tommy got the worst of it, but he broke away and ran off a few steps. "It isn't funny. My parents say the swamp water is poisonous."

"Your parents are stupid, LaChoy Boy. There's nothing wrong with the water. I've been in it before."

Tommy didn't say anything, just stared at Talmidge.

Talmidge looked at both of us. "Shit. Stay here then. We're going to the Big Mud."

Nose bloodied, Tommy watched Talmidge and Billy Booley started away down the boardwalk.

"Tommy," I nodded at his nose, "you okay?"

Still staring after Talmidge and Billy Booley, he used his shirt to wipe his nose and whispered, "Asshole."

I just shrugged. "Nobody can tell Talmidge anything he doesn't already know. He never listens to anybody. You know that."

He finally looked at me. "You want to go back to the colony?"

"What for?"

"Well …." He looked after Talmidge.

"I'm not afraid of him. I still want to see the bulliwogs." Unless …. "Did he lie about them being there?"

"No. They're there. I've seen them," Tommy said. "You sure?"

"Yeah. Let's go."

"Okay," he shrugged his brows and we followed the others down the board walk.

Talmidge only does that kind of stuff to try to keep me from hanging around. As long as I don't give in or cry, he always leaves me alone for a while. Anyway, I think he likes it better when I don't give in. It's like I'm proving I can take it. In some twisted way, Talmidge sort of respects that.

So, Tommy and me headed down the board walk after Talmidge and Billy Booley, sneakers clunking along the rubber coated, plastic treads the biologists laid down on the swamp. Otherwise, we would be up to our rears in those swimming-twitchy things and muck. The truth is, we weren't even supposed to walk down to the Big Mud at all without adults. Even then, we never used the board walk, that was for the biologists. We took hovers. Sometimes, Talmidge gets a good idea to do something, so you just go along with him, because that's what you do with Talmidge. You go along with him.

Keeping an eye on the backs of Talmidge's and Billy's bobbing heads, Tommy asked me, "so how do you like Shiners so far?"

I rolled my eyes at him. "You mean besides the smell."

Talmidge ripped off a huge mouth fart. "Must be the frogs."

We all laughed. It was a good one; peeled off long and really, really wet like someone farting out a poop. Billy Booley got laughing so hard, he grabbed his wiener through his shorts and staggered several steps before he got control of himself. Talmidge grabbed him by the back of the shirt and shook him around, "Don't whiz on yourself, Billy. Don't whiz on yourself."

Billy laughed so hard, tears started running down his face.

Talmidge kept jerking him back and forth, "Don't whiz! Don't whiz!" until Billy got mad, swore at Talmidge and jerked away to run ahead a few steps. That's Talmidge. He always has to take things a little too far. Nothing can ever be pure fun with him. He always has to be a little mean about stuff. He always has to spoil things a little.

Billy Booley is probably the only kid in school who is a big enough idiot to put up with him all the time. Almost as soon as Billy cursed off Talmidge, he fell into step right next to him again, competing with Talmidge for the best armpit fart and giggling about frogs.

I really didn't care what they did, as long as we went to the Big Mud. I wanted to see the bulliwogs. I read all about them on the transport that brought us to Shiners. So, me and Tommy clunked along behind Talmidge and Billy, keeping just far enough back to make it too much of a pain for them to turn around and bother us. Watching the back of Talmidge's head, Tommy said, "If you came all the way from Earth, then you must made most of the trip cryo."

"Yeah. So?"

He shrugged, "What was it like? In cryo, I mean?"

"Like being a popsicle, Asshole." Talmidge scoffed, "What do you think?"

Billy Booley giggled. "Yeah, Assss-hole. A popsicle."

Tommy ignored them and looked at me. "Well?"

"There's nothing to remember, except going to sleep and waking up. My hands were sort of tingly for a few days after I woke up." Talmidge muttered something dirty about being tingly, but I ignored him and told Tommy, "After we woke up we boarded a big transport and stayed there about four weeks until it reached Shiners."

"Yeah, " Tommy looked up through the hazy tree tops, "you can see the ships come into orbit on a clear night."

"When the air isn't full of swamp farts." Talmidge said over his shoulder. He squinted at Tommy. "Jeeesis, La Choy Boy, you gonna kiss her or what?"

Tommy blushed.

Talmidge was always ranking on Tommy like that, like he couldn't be friends with me, or just talk to me about stuff. When Tommy finally looked up from the board walk again, I pointed my index and pinkie fingers at Talmidge, making devil horns at the back of his head. Tommy went one better, and made double devil horns for both of them with both hands. We giggled.

Talmidge looked over his shoulder again. He squinted but he didn't do anything. We dropped our hands too fast for him to catch us.

When he kept staring over his shoulder, I ignored him and told Tommy, "Transport was boring anyway. All I ever did was look at disks on Shiners and the stuff the colony scientists are doing here."

"You miss Earth?"

I did, but I wasn't going to say so. It would have set Talmidge off for sure. "Shiners is sort of like Louisiana." That's where me and my parents came from. Except, the sky here isn't so much blue as a kind of dirty white. It's like a Louisiana summer all year round here being all the time sticky and warm, but the air is safe to breathe, and there are trees and grass and water, lots of water. "It's okay here."

"It sucks here." Talmidge snapped. He hated Shiners. Come to think of it, he spent a lot of time trying to make everyone else hate it, too. What he especially hates is the Big Mud. Tommy told me once that Talmidge almost drowned in it when he first came here. That was Talmidge's own fault. He tried walking on it by tying tennis rackets on his feet like snow shoes on snow or something. Well, it didn't work. He not only almost drowned, but he got in trouble for stealing those tennis rackets from the recreation concourse in Shiners Center.

Suddenly, Talmidge charged away at a dead run toward a bunch of thorn trees ahead of us. He jumped, shrieking, "Eeyaa!" and kicked off a thorn longer than he was tall, then scooped it up. He shook the thorn at the tree, shouting and pounding his skinny chest like a caveman. Billy laughed, then charged the tree and yelled, "Eeyaa!" and kicked off another thorn. They ran ahead shouting, "Bulliwogs!"

Looking ahead of them, I saw the gravy brown Big Mud stretch way out beyond the trees, but I couldn't make out anything floating on the surface from here.

Tommy shrugged at me, picked up a long thorn from the ground and trotted after the others. I did the same, not being tall enough to kick a one off the tree. As I ran passed, I noticed the wounded tree oozed white stuff.

The board walk ended where the swamp opened up to a long stretch of beach. It's the only solid piece of land on the other side of the swamp. From there the Big Mud goes on forever, all the way to the sunset. That mud is evil stuff, too. You can't walk on it, because it'll suck you down in a snap. It's so thick and heavy, little pools of water get pushed up to the surface. They scatter across the Big Mud all the way out to the horizon like thousands of glittering silver coins.

Tommy looked out over the seeping, brown sludge beyond the beach. "The cow is gone."

Last week one of the Holsteins broke out of the livestock graze area up in the Agrow. She wandered down here and got stuck. The farmers did everything they could think of to free that cow. Even my parents flew out with the big research foil. They used it to work out on the Mud all the time doing tests and stuff. They threw a rope around the cow and tried to pull her out. They almost tore her in half. She thrashed around and mooed sort of strangled and hoarse. Other kids came down with their parents who came to try to help. Some of them turned away covering their ears. Some even cried.

The Big Mud wasn't giving up that cow. That was all. So a man came with a rifle and shot her in the head. I guess that was better than letting her drown.

Talmidge saw that and said, "Man, I'd like to do that to this shit hole." He pointed his finger like a gun and cocked his thumb, aiming in it at the ground, then his thumb snapped forward and he made a noise like the gun was going off. Billy Booley giggled. I just felt a little sick to my stomach listening to the silence, because I could still hear that cow mooing in my head. Talmidge. He didn't think a thing about that poor cow. He doesn't think a thing for anybody.

Looking around, I noticed him and Billy Booley were already half way down the beach. They stopped beside one of those silvery pools. There was a cluster of what looked like billowy, yellow mushrooms about the size of watermelons. Some were bigger. Some were smaller. They bobbled in the up well current of the pool.

Talmidge stood there, pointing his thorn at them and announced, "Bulliwogs."

"I know that. I read all about them."

He sneered, "'I read all about them.' But you never saw a real one before."

I shrugged as I walked toward him and Billy, looking along the edge of the beach for whatever might be left of that cow. She was definitely gone. Sucked down, I guess.

"You know what we do with bulliwogs?"

I shrugged again, but I realized why Talmidge really wanted to come down here. I realized why he knocked a thorn off the tree. I realized why we all had them now. My stomach flip-flopped.

"We-" he raised his thorn high in both hands and brought it down, spearing a bulliwog. "Aaah!" He roared. The bulliwog shuddered. When Talmidge yanked his spear out, the bulliwog gushed a fountain of yellow stuff like cream of corn soup. It smelled like pee.

Billy Booley laughed and laughed until tears spurted out of his eyes. Tommy Choi just stepped back, wrinkling his whole face and muttered, "Gross," which was kind of what I was thinking.

"You better stop that, Talmidge." I should've known better. He never listens to any body. "What if its mother shows up?"

"These things don't have a mother." He laughed, watching the bulliwog ooze as it turned away and tried to paddle out of his reach. He pushed his spear into the hole in its back and dragged it toward him. It gave out a little croaking sound. He speared it again, grinning, and lifted it out of the pool, drizzling cream-of-corn soup blood, while it shuddered and wiggled and began to peep. Loud.

The hair on my arms stood up.

Billy laughed, "I never heard them make that sound before."

Talmidge shook the bulliwog off his spear onto the bank. "What the…?."

I backed away, watching the mud. "It's calling to its mother, Talmidge."

Talmidge sneered at me. "Call your mother." He muttered, "Stupid girl." Looking at me, he stabbed that bulliwog again. It went quiet.

Billy Booley laughed like an idiot. Tommy Choi didn't say a word.

All the sudden, the other bulliwogs started croaking. One by one, they started up. They got louder and louder until some of them started peeping. Pretty soon they were all peeping. Loud.

Still backing away, I shouted, "Talmidge! Stop it!"

Tommy Choi looked back over his shoulder at me. His eyes were so wide that I knew he read something about bulliwogs, too. All the sudden, he was right there with me, backing up the beach, getting away from the edge of the mud.

Even he shouted, "Talmidge, you better stop."

"Go kiss your girl friend, La Choy Boy."

Well, Talmidge wasn't about to stop. He was too mad and started spearing bulliwogs right and left. I guess he was trying to make them shut up. He threw them up on the bank where they kept peeping and spewing creamy yellow blood and flipping around on their backs, flippers going like mad in the air. That idiot Billy Booley ran around in circles, poking them and giggling.

That's when she came up. She burst from the pool, throwing a spray of mud and water across the beach. She was bigger than the pop up me and my parents lived in. And that had six rooms. She just brushed her babies aside as she threw her big, round belly on the bank, then planted her clawed flippers to hold her in place. Through her skin, I could see some of her insides. That cow that got stuck in the mud last week was all squashed up in her first stomach. Mostly horns and bone was all that was left.

The two tiny, shiny black eyes on the top of bulliwog's head didn't even look for Talmidge and Billy Booley, she just seemed to know where exactly they were. They started to turn toward the sound of her wet body slapping on the bank, but they weren't nearly quick enough. Her wide mouth opened and, with a quick nod, she snapped it closed on them both, then slid down the bank. A second later, the pool was still again, except for a fresh whirl of mud where the mother bulliwog went down.

And that was it.

She snatched those boys off the beach and left nothing behind but their muddy sneakers. The only sound on all of Shiners, was the tiny lap-lap of those baby bulliwogs as they paddled back into the pool. Tommy and me just stood there. Maybe neither one of us knew what to do. Maybe we were in shock. All I know is that I noticed how peaceful and quiet it suddenly was with those two boys gone. I didn't feel bad about Talmidge one bit. I didn't feel bad about that idiot Billy Booley either.

After a while, Tommy said, "Why couldn't he just listen for once?"

"Talmidge didn't listen to anybody." I noticed those empty sneakers sticking out of the mud all cockeyed.

And now? I guess he never will.

Published in: *GateWay Science Fiction*, Summer 2002; *Aphelion Science Fiction Webzine*, August 2001

SOLAR MAX

Ignoring the hard shimmy from the engines, Reggie pulled her belts tighter and focused on the sensor console that wrapped around her seat like a black crescent moon. The panel that monitored the heat shields on the belly of the Felix went dark.

It meant that Maxwell dipped too close to the last flare. A hundred miles above the edge of the event, the temperature was still close to half a million degrees Kelvin. Blind underneath, she couldn't tell whether the tiles absorbed the blast or if the belly of the Felix was about to disintegrate in ashes under them.

Glancing at the rest of the panels, she didn't see any panic lights flashing. None of the environmental sirens had gone off. They were okay so far.

Voice rattling with the ship, Reggie snapped over her throat mike, "Damn it, Maxwell, I just lost the heat shield sensors. Stop screwing around."

His cackle crackled through her ear piece. "Relax, Reggie."

"Max, you can't keep blowing through the ass end of the events like that. The Felix is getting burned."

"We're fine."

The Felix's shaking tapered off as they escaped solar gravity. Reggie keyed up one of the satellite cameras that orbited Sol and toggled it to swing toward the ship. An H-alpha filter dropped over the lens automatically, tinting the sun ruby red as it filled the frame. She saw the ship glimmer pinkly as it arced above the red sun. Like all dipper ships it was a sleek, portal-less black bullet; covered in layer upon layer of radiation shielding and ceramic composites and studded with sensor pores from nose to stern. It arced above the roiling photosphere like a dark shark circling in bright, bloody depths.

"Maxwell, make a fly-by on camera six-niner-six."

"What for?"

"I want to see how bad we're scorched."

"None of the panic lights are flashing."

"They wouldn't if you scorched the sensors. Just do it. I'm not sure we'll make it back to the carrier without breaking up."

He muttered something about ". . . so melodramatic," over the mike.

"Maxwell..." Reggie growled, eyeing the screen to make sure the Felix swung toward the camera.

Maneuvering thrusters began to fire. Reggie relaxed in her seat, bobbling a little in her belts. Maxwell must have been on his best behavior today because of their charter. He usually argued more.

"Captain D'Oro?"

Reggie looked up from the progress on the monitor. Arnold Nichols drifted in the hatchway. He peered out from the steel rims taped to his temples to keep them from floating away. "Yes, Doctor?"

"Why are we moving away from the study area?"

"Safety check."

Face turning pale, the good doctor licked his lips and

grabbed an over head glide rail to steady his drift. "Is every thing all right?"

"Routine after such a close pass." It wasn't, but there was no use in panicking Nichols. The man obviously was here for the science, not the excitement of space travel. "That scopolamine patch working for you?"

"Yes, I believe it is." He touched his nape where the patch was. "I'm not as dizzy now. Thank you."

Something scraped heavily over the Felix's hull.

"Oh," said Doctor Nichols, turning as white as his flight suit. His eyes lifted toward the ceiling, seeking the source of the noise.

The scrape ended in a soft whine, then silence filled the sensor module.

Maxwell crackled. "Oops. What was that, Reggie?"

Reggie growled internally as she dropped her eyes to the monitor. There was nothing but blackened tiles in the frame, so she toggled the camera and spotted the bright outline of the satellite's radio antenna bent across the silhouette of the hull. Reggie noticed Nichols looking moist as he clutched the ceiling gliderail. She pressed the receiver tighter to her ear to make sure none of Max's response leaked out for the doctor to hear. "A bent satellite antenna."

Maxwell groaned. "That'll piss off the Consortium. Are we hung up on it?"

"I don't think so. A couple of burns will lift us off it."

"How's our tummy look, Reggie? Are we singed?" Reggie toggled the camera, rolling the view up and down the tiles.

"Everything looks like it's intact."

"Told ya'."

Reggie gritted her teeth. At times like this she wanted to chuck the Felix, Maxwell, her contract; the whole friggin' mess and semi-retire earth side, maybe pick up some consulting gig with one of the marketing firms like Space, Inc. They called her once and she almost went, but being out here so close to the power and beauty of the sun ... well, there was nothing else like it.

For now, Reggie still wanted to be exactly where she was no matter the risks.

"What, Reg? No smart ass come back?"

Or, the aggravation. "Doctor Nichols is here with me."

"Ooooh." Maxwell chuckled. "Good thing he can't hear me."

"Good thing," Reggie said, winking at the nauseous looking doctor.

Taking her remark as good news, Nichols's smile twitched to life.

"So what's the verdict, Reg?" She could almost hear Maxwell's grin through her ear phone, "Do we continue or abort?"

Reggie eyed Nichols. They needed this contract.

If she aborted now, the doctor and his group might go else where. They weren't likely to reschedule after today's performance. Worse, the Consortium gave her a one shot deal.

Make this expedition work or resume subcontracting tourist tours. The board wasn't convinced there was as much money in chartering research groups as there was in chartering tourists. They were probably right.

Judging by the amount of dew on Nichols's upper lip, Maxwell's *yee-ha* flying style didn't fill the doctor with confidence.

They would be back to ferrying tourists which Max loved. He kept track of the number of solar tours they flew by the number of lays he scored. He loved slathering their charters with charm; hand kissing all the heiresses, actresses and super models that crossed the threshold of the Felix. They loved his cocky grin and his sun bleached blonde surfer-dude mop of hair. He played the winsome rake very well, but playing tour boat captain grated on Reggie. She wanted more prestige. The scientific excursions gave her that and Maxwell could still play the brainiacs like a cruise director. Beside, he wasn't as reckless with a charter of researchers as he sometimes was with the tourists. He couldn't resist dazzling the ladies with some borderline dangerous maneuvers.

Either way, expedition was a wash. If they stayed, they jeopardized the scientists. There was no way to tell how badly damaged the Felix was until they returned to the carrier for an inspection. If Maxwell decided to go corona surfing again, maybe one more blast would cook the belly off the ship. If Reggie aborted, she had a feeling she would loose the Nichols expedition permanently. Reggie groaned as her conscience snatched away her last, best opportunity for respectability.

"We're aborting."

"You've got no balls, Reg."

"You've got too many, Maxwell."

He laughed.

Reggie watched the monitor as the Felix fired thrusters to lift gently away from the camera. The radio antenna scraped against the hull for a moment until it slid clear.

"What is that?" Nichols gulped, eyes darting back anforth.

"Nothing to worry about, Doctor."

Then the ship fell quiet. Reggie felt the engines boost a moment as Max ignited them to make some velocity toward the carrier.

Anxieties seeming to quiet again, the doctor looked at Reggie. "Did you say something about aborting?"

"I'm sorry, Doctor, but we took a lot of heat on that last pass. I rather err on the side of caution. We're heading back to the carrier for an inspection."

Nichols nodded, releasing the gliderail long enough to wipe his wet lip. "Best to be cautious, Captain D'Oro."

Desperate not to loose the business Reggie told him, "You're welcome to place another charter voucher on the carrier. I'll be happy to honor a return trip so that you can finish your experiments in the morning. No additional charge."

"If the Felix passes inspection."

"Of course, pending the inspection."

"We'll see how it goes." He glided out.

Reggie sighed. Nichols would have another charter before morning. Maxwell blew it. She wanted to strangle him.

The post flight check behind her, Reggie over handed down the empty docking sleeve still mumbling about Maxwell when laughter erupted from the boarding vestibule ahead. She winced. No doubt her pilot gave a glib recounting of the disastrous flight to the other dipper jocks. As she floated out of the sleeve, she found Maxwell surrounded by the researchers, not his cocky stick jockey pals. The group chuckled along with him. Nichols's color was better. He smiled along with the others.

She hung back in the mouth of the sleeve, trying not to taint the moment. It looked like Maxwell had them on the edge of not canceling the charter.

He told Nichols, "Anyway, Doc, if you stay at the Hilton, make sure to ask for Mona. She's the best masseuse in Sol system."

Grating aggravation began to disintegrate as Reggie watched her pilot work the room. He was a borne public relations man.

"I will, Maxwell." Nichols smiled easily, looked relaxed and reassured. "And thank you. We'll see you in the morning then."

"In the morning." Maxwell gave him a crisp salute, hawk eyed and deadly serious, then he winked.

The doctor chuckled as he saluted back, then he and his group pushed off and over handed down the gain way tube to the carrier ring.

Reggie over handed into the vestibule. "Tell me you saved the charter."

"I saved the charter," Maxwell grinned.

Reggie gritted her teeth, glad and mad at the same time. Whatever Maxwell dug himself into, he always seemed to be able to dig himself out of. It was soooo wrong. And yet, it served her needs. How could she argue?

The truth was, the Consortium should've bumped Maxwell from the cockpit months ago, but he was the first and only NASA pilot they recruited. Granted, he was a washout; got dumped from the program half way through his training because they labeled him a discipline problem. He couldn't resist buzzing the spoke towers on the tori habitats over Venus. He would have been a good pilot, maybe a great pilot if the theme song `I Did It My Way' didn't perpetually play in his head. It didn't matter. The Consortium liked him. He was a handsome, charasmatic pitchman. "Okay. How'd you do it?"

Maxwell drifted toward her, slowly rolling onto his back as he clasped his hands behind his head and crossed his ankles like he was stretching out on an invisible couch. "I told `em that whether they take another charter or not, they might as well leave their equipment on the Felix tonight, rather than go to the bother of off loading it because nobody would be around to on load it onto another vessel until morning. Unless, they wanted to risk it being stolen, they would have to pay for storage some place on the carrier. By then, the Felix will be certified by the night crew and she'll be ready to fly again. They won't have wasted money on storage."

"That's it?"

His smile turned sheepish.

"What else, Maxwell?"

"We're putting them up at the Hilton tonight."

"We're paying for the entire group to stay in the Hilton?"

He shrugged. "'It was only the thing I could think of to keep `em interested."

Reggie groaned. That would take a big, ugly bite out of their commission. She eyed Maxwell. Correction. *His* commission. "Well, you botched the trip and you offered the hotel to them, so the charges for the rooms come out of your percentage."

Maxwell shrugged a shoulder. "Yeah. Sure. Whatever." He rolled upright, catching the gliderail overhead. "Hey, go for nightcap at Sunspot's?"

Reggie lifted a brow. "After the way you almost blew this trip? I ought to tear you a new one, Maxwell. No. I don't want to go for a nightcap with you."

He shrugged his brows. "Suit yourself." He pushed off for the gainway. "See ya' at zero six hundred, Reggie."

Implacably blonde and always smiling; that was the image of Maxwell that stuck with Reggie as he glided down the throat of the gain-way. She unclenched her jaws. The truth was she could've used that drink.

The idea of selling her contract and getting out of the business crept into her thoughts again. Maybe the exotic flavor of sun dipping was wearing thin after all, but something else remained; a vague sense of dread. Reggie realized that she was a little afraid to leave. The truth was that Maxwell was reckless in the cockpit. She had the nagging feeling that if she wasn't there to catch his mistakes, he would get people killed sooner or later.

She groaned, wondering if she was too much of a hard ass. Sunspot's wasn't a bad idea. Have a few drinks, have a few laughs and forget today ever happened. After all, things worked out even if it was the usual cockeyed, inside out way things always did when Max was involved. Max's phenomenal luck never seemed to run out. All anyone could do was stand back and watch in astonishment. Maxwell was like a trapeze artist working the high wire without a net. He just seemed to know instinctively that he was never going to fall. Who couldn't admire that just a little.

Reggie pushed off, caught the gliderail and over handed down the bright gain-way. "Maxwell, wait up."

Pressing her receiver tightly to her ear, Reggie gazed at the same monitor as Nichols. He had called her to the research module to observe. She had no idea what she was looking at, but Nichols was very excited and wanted to share. So Reggie smiled and nodded, while he rattled on about his experiments. She found herself almost wishing for the giddy, mindless banter of martini sipping debutants again.

Maxwell could hear the doctor through her throat mike and couldn't resist a running commentary. "Sheesh, Reg, tell him to shut up already. I'm dozing off up here."

Unable to respond without insulting their charter, she answered, "Copy that, Pilot."

Doctor Nichols barely paused in his description of the experiment his staff ran, but touched Reggie's arm to refocus her attention on the screen.

The filtered sun, glowing like a backlit ruby filled the frame, was plotted out on a blue-luminous grid in kilometers.

"What's terribly exciting," the doctor said, "are the redundancy ratios we've been calculating."

"Redundancy ratios?"

"Oh, yes. Of the flares. We're finding that the events cycle in sets. Certain events hiccup. It's quite remarkable and the principles we're learning about plasma mechanics will have far reaching implications in the energy management industry and even propulsion."

"I know I'd like to launch him about now," Maxwell crackled.

Reggie resisted a smile. She might have shut off her headset, but it was forbidden by Consortium operating procedure and the Felix's com system recorded such breaches.

"Sol has a quite consistent internal clock when it comes to combustion. We are beginning to track the pattern of the disturbances as they rise into the photosphere. We plot the flares by monitoring the build up of electromagnetic flux on the surface.

That means we could place monitoring stations alongside plasma turbines in solar orbit to extract the energy from the flares then transfer the power to any of the stations, ring habitats or colonies in the solar system. Think of the resources!"

"Think of the boredom." Max snickered in her ear. "Reg, I feel a loop-de-loop coming on."

Reggie frowned. Maxwell must have been one of those kids who could never sit still in the back of the classroom. "Copy that, Pilot. Maintain your position. We're tracking an event."

Doctor Nichols blinked at her. "Is something wrong, Captain D'Oro?"

"Just a routine maneuver check from the cockpit."

"Oh." He looked gravely over the tops of his sinking-rising silver rims, "It is crucial we maintain a stable orbit, Captain D'Oro. Even at this altitude over Sol, there is considerable risk."

"No need for concern, Doctor Nichols. Everything is under control."

He smiled. "Very well." Then nodded to the display, "As you can see, we're about to record another disharge. See the spike building here," He pointed to the new graph superimposed on the screen. The spike liquidly jumped up the axis points. "That's a new magnetic arc building at the eruption sight. Spectacular, isn't it?"

"Well, I ."

"Aaaah!" Nichols said, "There's the first volley."

The arc vanished and plasma erupted out of the photosphere of the sun.

"Oh, brother. Enough already." Max groaned. "Hold tight!"

"The hiccup volley will follow close behind," Nichols said, gleaming eyes locked on the screen.

The Felix shimmied briefly, kicking off Sol's gravity as it peeled out of its holding pattern.

"Maxwell!" Reggie snapped.

The scientists tumbled away lazily from their stations, looking perplexed as they sprawled in near zero G.

Nichols's mouth fell open as he flailed for a hand hold, first making a grab for the brow of the monitor and then for the bulkhead over head. "Captain D'Oro!"

Reggie just tucked in her arms and legs, frowning as the Felix rolled around them, while the cowboy in the cockpit hooted in her ear. His debutants would have loved it. As for her researchers; some of them saw her posture and adopted the same positions. Poor Nichols bumped his head on the floor before he found something to cling to.

As the Felix pulled out of the loop, Reggie realized what Max was doing. He wanted to sabotage this expedition. He wanted the tourist runs back; his captive audience of dazzled heiresses, actresses and super models. Why wouldn't he?

"Son of a bitch," Reggie snarled as she started clawing her way through the research module forward toward the glideway to the cockpit. She was going to kill Maxwell with her bare hands.

"Captain D'Oro!" Nichols shouted.

Just as she turned back to see him clutching the console monitor in both hands, static roared through her ear piece. The noise scraping over her ear drum brought tears to her eyes. The pain quit with her grimace.

"The redundancy!" Nichols gasped.

He didn't have to say anything more. A gust of heat rolled down the glideway from the cockpit and stole Reggie's breath.

Hull breach sirens went off forward, then another set went off in the glideway to the cockpit. Reggie plunged back into the research module. She ignored the emergency protocol to secure the hatch to the glideway and cockpit. There wasn't time.

Sirens went off in the research module. She twisted toward the researchers; all stunned with their mouths open, eyes wide, floating like drowning victims even though they weren't dead. Yet. "Everybody aft. Into the sensor module."

She would cut the sensor module loose from the dipper if she had to. With the hull breached, the distress beacon had already begun to signal. A rescue ship from the carrier was already launching.

The Felix began to lose attitude. The spin was slow, but the scientists had some difficulty handling it as they made for the aft module.

Heat building rapidly behind her, Reggie pushed them ahead of her. "Go."

"Your pilot!"

There wasn't time to worry about Maxwell. "Go!" she snapped, shoving the slower ones, herding her quivering charter down the aft glideway to the sensor module.

She followed, turning to seal the hatch to the research module. Far up the glideway, the circular entrance to the research module glowed orange and rippled like a hot oven.

They didn't have much time. Maybe they didn't have any. Reggie slammed the lock closed, spun the wheel and secured it. The safety light above it changed from red to green.

Twenty one people huddled in the slowly revolving module while Reggie strapped in. She swallowed the panic that knotted in her throat when she saw all the lights flashing on her panels. She slapped off the audio alarms, then keyed up the control panel. The console already showed the over-ride for the Felix's controls had been rerouted to the aft module. It meant whatever was forward of their module was already frying.

She tried not to think of Maxwell. The cockpit was cooked by now.

Eying the gyroscope to make sure their spin was manageable, Reggie keyed the releases on the clamps on the research module and cockpit, then listened with the rest of the ears in the sensor module as it released from the dipper.

She would have preferred to slow their rotation before disengaging, but there wasn't time. With the forward sections of the Felix burned, the sensor module had to get clear before gravity pulled the entire vessel toward the corona where the heat would evaporate everything. The Felix's aft section broke away with a soft, scraping *clunk*.

Glancing at the researchers huddled together on the ceiling gliderail like pale bats, Reggie marked their position, then fired thrusters, lifting them gently away from the rest of the ship, then keyed up one of the cameras.

On her screen, the forward section of the Felix glowed brightly as it began to tip toward the corona. Reggie swallowed.

Maxwell was already dead.

It evaporated in mid dive, leaving nothing but the graceful, luminous trail of its ghost behind at high above the corona. A few seconds later and that dissolved, too.

She noticed her charter still clustered on the ceiling, too terrified to move. "Everybody alright?"

They looked at one another. Nichols adjusted his cockeyed glasses. "Yes. I believe we are."

Reggie nodded, noticed their trajectory on the console and fired the thrusters again. Her ear piece crackled. For an instant hope leaped in her chest, then she realized that it couldn't be Maxwell. He was dead.

"Carrier Dispatch to Felix. We're receiving a distress signal. Over."

"Felix to Carrier Dispatch. Over. We've had an accident.

The sensor module is secure, but we require rescue."

"Carrier Dispatch. Understood. We're sending a recovery unit to your coordinates. ETA thirty minutes. Over." "Felix sensor module. Roger that, Dispatch. We'll be fine until then. Over."

She told her stunned charter. "They're coming."

Reggie eased back in her seat, bobbling in her belts and noticed the screen. Where the Felix disintegrated, space seemed more empty than she ever remembered it being. In the photosphere plasma boiled where the dipper ship went down.

For the first time Reggie looked at the sun and didn't see the majesty of it. It was just a ball of raw and godless power. At least, she was sure Maxwell didn't feel much. It looked like the forward sections caught the brunt of the redundant discharge, so he was probably incinerated instantly. It was one situation Maxwell couldn't dig himself out of.

She squeezed her eyes tight, but could still see the flash of his cocky grin. In a weird way, Maxwell got the last laugh. There would be no more science charters. There would be no more charters of any kind. Reggie's ship was destroyed. Along with it, probably her reputation and her contract with the Consortium. At least now she had an excuse to resign. Returning to Earth might be her only option. Feeling heavy as lead, she still didn't sink into her seat.

Then... thumping came from the airlock to the sensor module.

Everyone looked at it.

At first, Reggie thought it was debris bumping against the glideway that was still attached to the sensor module, but the sound repeated too rhythmically. Thump-thump-thump. Then harder. *Thump. Thump. Thump.*

"God," Nichols gasped, "Someone's in the glideway."

He started toward the airlock.

Reggie tore out of her belts. "Don't touch it." She pushed off toward the lock, glancing over the gages to make sure the entire glideway was pressurized and secure. She had left the outer lock wide open. To her surprise, the glideway was pressurized and secure. That meant someone closed the other lock.

She spun the wheel releasing the hatch cover, planted her feet on the wall and pulled it open.

Maxwell spilled in, gold hair and head set melted into his blister pocked, lobster red skin. He gasped for air through his grimace.

Glancing down the glideway, Reggie saw that he managed to close the safety lock at the far end, making the aft glideway a cozy little life pod. Still the effects of his egress through that oven hot research module were obvious. His eye lashes and eye brows were gone. His ears had melted. His flight suit was mostly burned off. His hands were badly burned, already swollen like oven mitts. His fingers were blackened and withered. Reggie grabbed him under the arms and pulled him in.

Grinning in pain, he rasped, "Sorry about your ship,

Reggie." He started to laugh, but coughed instead and passed out.

"Maxwell," Reggie gritted her teeth, glad and mad at the same time. Whatever Maxwell dug himself into, he always seemed to be able to dig himself out of.

This time, she didn't mind.

TOBIAS UNBOUND

The first time I met Tobias Herman, he was spit polishing the brass plaque beside the archway to the arboretum. Spit polishing it. I never saw anyone spit polish anything before but there he was, gripping the hallway glide bar with one hand to steady himself against the sphere's lazy knack for gravity while he vigorously rubbed saliva into the edges of the 'R' in Roosa of the Stuart Roosa Arboretum plaque with a soggy rag.

It was such a quaint behavior that I paused to watch him. He was a slightly built, little man with a sloppy mop of black hair made more unruly by low G. Everything about him, his smallness, his pastel demeanor seemed inadequate to meet the demands of the sphere's environment.

His furious polishing slowed as he sensed me watching. After a moment, he turned his head so that one brown eye glimmered at me over the top of his pale coverall shoulder. He watched me out of that eye without introducing himself, though fresh color crept up his cheek. Indeed, he did not speak at all. He almost never spoke unless he was spoken to first. Eventually, I discovered it was part of his illness.

At the time, I didn't know Tobias Herman at all, so I smiled and mistakenly assumed, "You must be the new janitor."

Mouth hidden by his shoulder, he answered with a muffled, "Botanist."

"Oh yes," I chuckled, "You must be Mr. Herman."

His brown eye held me. It was all the acknowledge-ment he could muster.

I had been expecting him to arrive today. Tobias Herman had an impressive background in low G hydro-ponics. He was the lead botanical engineer on the design team who created the root mats we installed in our arboretum six months ago. The same mats that have been so successful on the moon colonies. According to the recommendation attached to his application, he was the one who proposed the design. The results here have been astonishing. Naturally, when he applied for the job opening I hired him sight unseen. The sphere needed Tobias's kind of talent. I stepped toward him offering my hand. "I'm John."

Tobias hesitated, glimpsing at my open hand. His grip on the plaque seemed to tighten.

"John Shepherd."

He kept staring.

"The director."

Tobias blinked.

"... Of the arboretum." I kept my hand out there, having already gathered that Tobias was a slightly odd bird. No doubt he was the kind of man who preferred the quiet company of his research to people. His eccentric nature was no bother. The exotic nature of sphere living attracts an assortment of personalities, but they all came with talent and a penchant for adventure. Those were the bonds that make us all family here.

A flicker of etiquette softened the doubt in his dark eyes. He tucked the rag in his hip pocket before he took my hand. Ignoring the singularly organic dampness of his grip, I shook with him then tossed a nod at the gleaming plaque and told him, "Nice shine there."

Tobias noticed at the plaque.

"You're right on time. I'm just coming in open the gardens for the day. I'll give you a little tour then we'll get you started."

Gravipeds holding us to the floor, we scuffled along the gleaming, translucent ribbon of the Grand Walk that arched over the reservoir to the bowl of the arboretum. "May I call you 'Toby'?"

Tobias's mouth braced faintly. "I rather you didn't."

"'Tobias' then?"

He made no remark.

"Alright Tobias it is." We stopped at the iris lock to the arboretum. Lifting the cover on the control panel, I thumbed the pad and watched the iris, painted as red petals, unfurl. Our resident muralist did the work. Each morning the arboretum opens like a rose.

Green lawns and the meandering boughs of fruit trees sprawled before us.

We passed through onto the walkway that curved through the lawns and under the trees of the public gardens. The imported moon bricks in the walk sparkled like new driven snow.

Gesturing to the rye sod on either side of the brick way, I told Tobias, "We've implemented your mat system here. The plants are knitting themselves into the netting nicely. We have to trim occasionally, but as long as we keep the drip and nutrient base running through the weep lines, they stay put. It's working so well that we are ordering more mats for production and seeding. I'm pushing the sphere development board to sod the entire sphere. I believe, Tobias, that once we attain hydrometric balance out in the rest of the sphere, we can turn off the drip system permanently. Look here." Excited now, I stopped, stooped and lifted an edge of the mat careful not to pull on the bolts that secured it to the foundation of the dome. "Humus! Tobias. We're building a humus layer under the mat."

His mouth twitched in anemic pride of the success.

We shuffled on. "You'll find that the colonists like to come down on their lunch hours. The park fills up with kids after three. School gets out and they like to come here to play. It's good PR so we don't mind, but they are restricted to the park area. If you see any of the teens trying bounce into the ceiling struts, don't hesitate to com security."

Tobias stopped and looked up. His mouth opened a little.

"Oh, they can't break the dome sections, but they could damage the light panels or get a nasty shock off the transformers if they grab the cable bundles up there."

Tobias nodded slightly, though he kept studying the ceiling.

I started forward again then noticed that he was not following, still transfixed by the ceiling for some reason. "Tobias?"

He looked at me. For an instant, his expression was blank. I almost wondered if he had forgotten who I was. "Come along."

He shuffled after me a little too slowly, brown eyes searching our girdered sky.

Passing alongside the tentacling branches of apple saplings, we headed toward the green houses. I introduced him to the rest of the staff, leading him down the row. Tobias was as diffident with his new coworkers as he was with me.

At last, I led him to his own green house. All the botanists have their own area. I encouraged them to experiment in addition to their regular duties. Frankly, Tobias's root mats are so successful that I couldn't help expecting great things from him.

As we reached his area, he seemed to brighten a little actually stepping ahead of me into the long hollow space of his green house. The opaque plastic walls let in light from the ceiling panels but it also had its own enormous ribbon of grow lights fastened to the PVC roof trusses. I watched a moment as Tobias played momentarily with the faucet levers on the irrigation net. His bush bean crop was already started. It filled the nets with vibrant green foliage. Many of the plants had already begun setting pods. He smiled faintly. I can't tell you how deeply that tiny acknowledgement pleased me. Tobias's relief became my own. I understood him quite well already. I appreciated his sweetly shy disposition. There was a quiet dignity about the man. He was content among plants, but it was clear to me that people were a source of quiet anxiety to him. To be honest, he reminded me of myself when I first arrived here.

The sphere has a way of drawing people out. I had a hunch it would do the same for Tobias. He needed us as much as we needed him. He made the right choice coming here. We would be good for him. The sphere would be good for him. And he would be good for us. "Tobias?"

He gave me that sweet, shy over-the-shoulder look again.

"May I ask what prompted you to leave the Moon to come here?"

He paused so long that I wondered whether he considered not answering, but his gaze drifted dreamily toward the ceiling and he uttered, "gravity."

I nodded, smiling, knowing him better by the minute in spite of his quiet nature. It was the challenge Tobias craved. Gravity here was but a whisper of what it was on the moon. A good push and a man would go sailing toward the center of the sphere. It was an environment meant to challenge the best and brightest. Clearly, Tobias was one of those.

I gave him the studies and maintenance schedule for his greenhouse then left him to revel in the comfortable solitude of his duties.

I had no reason to see Tobias again until the following Friday when I noticed that he hadn't e-mailed his weekly report as all the staff did at week's end. It was an oversight on his part, but it was little bother and I was eager to see how my retiring botanist had settled in, so I headed down the brick way to Tobias's area.

Passing the hearty green glow of produce through the plastic of the other greenhouses, I reached Tobias's area. Something was wrong there. Large patches of irrigation net pocked the green. Pausing to look in through the plastic sheeting, I saw Tobias's bush bean crop wilted on the nets. If there was trouble in the system or blight or some other problem, he should have reported it at once. I hurried to the doorway looked inside.

The plants were all miserably dehydrated, some possibly beyond rescue.

"Tobias?" His green house was quiet. "Tobias, are you here?"

Ventilation rattled the plastic walls softly, but no one answered. Just then I felt a stare and turned.

Tobias paused meekly in the doorway of his lab module, eyes pinched and black hair mussed. He looked to be in the same coveralls that he wore to work last Monday. At least, the garment looked as rumpled and dirty as if he had slept in it all week then I noticed the polishing rag from Monday still hanging from his hip pocket.

"Is everything alright here, Tobias?"

He nodded.

I noticed the green house full of wilting beans, but decided to start with first things first, "I came around to see how things were going. I missed your weekly report." I nodded at the beans, "Are you having a problem here?"

"No, Sir."

His answer perturbed me, so I insisted - gently - considering his mild nature. "But your control crop needs water, Tobias. Is the irrigation net functioning alright?"

"I believe so, Sir."

"Have you maintenanced it?"

Without answering, Tobias shuffled inside the unlit lab module. The darkness swallowed him.

Concerned for the crop, I went into the greenhouse, set the timers on the net so that the beans remained properly hydrated and fed then turned my attention to Tobias.

At the door of the lab module, I thumbed the light switch.

The moment the overhead flickered on, Tobias shirked where he stood in the back corner. His hands remained inert at his sides.

"I can't stress enough the importance of tending the control crop, Tobias."

"Yes, Sir," he said softly. The sound of humiliated apology in his voice doused my impatience with the man. He was desperately shy, but I was sure that with gentle handling, Tobias would come along. I knew that he would. Geniuses often have tender souls.

My shoulders dropping a little, I noticed the dark monitor on his workstation. "As for your report." I sat down, turned on the station and watched the monitor light up. It asked for a username and password. "What's your password, Tobias?"

He said nothing.

I looked at him.

He shrugged.

Realization struck me. Tobias wasn't being obstinate. The tech from IS hadn't come by to give him his password. How could he log his reports and maintain the greenhouse systems without access to the network? Of course, he couldn't. "Well, this must be the problem." I winked at him. "If you ever have a situation like this again, Tobias, don't hesitate to come tell me. I'll have IS come down and log you onto the system right away. You'll have a username and password before noon."

"Thank you, Sir."

I smiled, charmed by his formality as I turned on the chair to tell him, "Tobias, you can call me John."

"I rather not, Sir."

"Suit yourself." As I rose I noticed the rear of the lab module. There was a body sized indent on the top layer of the fertilizer sacks stacked along the left wall. A small pile of empty bean pods littered the floor. I could scarcely believe that Tobias might have been living here in his lab module and subsisting on bush beans for the passed week. It couldn't be true. "Are those bean pods, Tobias?"

"Yes, Sir."

I gestured to the sacks. "Have you been sleeping here all week?"

He swallowed and stared at me, then admitted the faintest nod.

"Wouldn't you prefer your cabin?"

"I rather sleep here, Sir."

"Your cabin would be so much more comfortable. And the beans, Tobias. Well, you can't keep eating from the study plants in green house. It simply won't do. Tonight you'll report to your quarters. Is that understood?"

"Yes, Sir."

"Trust me, Tobias, you'll be much more comfortable there." As I turned to leave I reminded him, "And don't forget your report."

"Yes, Sir."

I left him there standing in the door of the lab module confident that the situation would resolve itself, though I confess that I began to have doubts about Tobias's mental state. I wanted to give him a chance. He had only been here a week. After all, his only real crime so far was his persistent shyness. He might do better to have a session or two with a psychologist. Adapting to sphere living takes some adjusting. I myself experienced a mild bout of depression the first month or so that I arrived here. Terran bonds can be hard to break. My brother and two sisters still live on Earth. I might visit them more often if not for the expense of a ticket and the elaborate preparation time involved so that I could tolerate terran gravity again. After ten years in the arboretum, the sphere is home for me, but there are still moments that I miss my siblings and Earth.

It's why Roosa is so important to the colonists. I truly believe the arboretum is the reason we stay sane here. In time, with the help of green lawns, soaring fruit trees, rose bushes, plots of flowers, vegetables and so on; the most precious jewels from Earth, we were able to adjust. Like the rest of us, Tobias needed patience and the opportunity to prove himself. He deserved that much.

Monday morning I stared at my e-mail. Tobias's name was still missing from the list of late reports downloaded into my mailbox. While I bit the inside of my cheek and tried to muster a reason why he didn't respond, my com buzzed.

"Director Shepherd, I have Mary Kai from Residence Management on the line. Can you take the call?"

I gave my secretary the affirmative and he patched the call through. Mary appeared on my walltall. "John, here. Mary, how are you?"

"Well. Thank you, John." She was a charming, petite Asian woman in her very youthful fifties. "I'm calling to clarify your staff request for cabin space in the residence module."

"What about it?"

"When is ..." She glanced down to read off her palmtop, "Tobias C. Herman's ETA?"

My gut sank. I knew instantly what happened. Tobias never went to his cabin last Friday. Likely, he slept in the lab module all weekend. "I take it he never checked in there?"

She nodded. "I've had a cabin prepped and waiting for him for better than a week."

"Thank you, Mary. I'm afraid Tobias is having some trouble adjusting to sphere living."

"Then he's arrived?"

"Oh, he's here."

Her brow crinkled. Mary took a great deal of pride in managing the domestic comforts of the colonists. "Is he unhappy with his quarters?"

"No, no, nothing like that. I don't think he's actually seen it yet."

Her brow crinkled again. "Where is he staying?"

"Don't worry about that, Mary. I'll see that he moves in this evening."

Her smile returned. "I'll be sure to check in with him a little later in the week then to make sure he's settling in all right. Bye, John."

"Bye, Mary."

Sighing, I commed Tobias's lab module.

After a couple of hails, he stepped into view on my walltall looking more disheveled than he did on Friday. "Yes, Sir?"

"I still need your report, Tobias."

"Yes, Sir."

"Get to it, will you?"

"Yes, Sir."

"And, Tobias, I'll be around to see you at seventeen hundred. I thought we could have dinner together then I could walk you to your quarters and help you get settled in there."

He blinked.

"What do you say?"

"I ...."

"Yes, Tobias?"

"I rather not, Sir."

I chuckled taken back slightly. "You rather not do which, Tobias? Go to dinner with me? Or, go to your quarters?"

His mouth worked a moment then he said, "I rather not do either." Then softly, urgently he added, "Sir."

"Come on. It's my treat." I confess that I was already planning to refer him to the mental health clinic in the Health Services Annex. I joked, "You must be sick of bush beans by now."

Tobias never twitched a facial muscle, but simply stared at me.

I insisted, "I'll come around at seventeen hundred, Tobias. I'll see you then." It was not my intention to force myself on the poor fellow, but he was in desperate need of help. As his supervisor, I was duty bound to intervene for his own good.

Come quitting time, I shuffled down the brick way, under the madly curling branches of the apple trees toward the greenhouses.

Out in the garden, children bounded across the rye grass like gazelles. They're the ones who knew how to make the most of the environment here. They delighted in low gravity, treating the sphere like a giant trampoline. Acrobatics was the most popular sport among the middle schoolers and the teens. They were quite graceful, leaping, somersaulting and pin wheeling about. Catching sight of them as they frolicked like lighter-than-air nymphs lifted my mood as I approached Tobias's area.

The sight of flourishing bush beans in his green house reassured me a bit. Although I noticed that he had neglected to weed out the few plants that withered under the previous week of neglect. Still, I was confident that Tobias was beginning to come around at last. Of course, I knew that he would.

I stopped inside briefly to check the auto settings on the system to make sure all of the nets were getting adequate water and nutrients, saw that they were fine and went to the lab module.

The door was closed, so I knocked. "Tobias?" I tapped again. "Tobias, it's John. Are you ready to go?" It was then that I noticed the crease between the door and the threshold was dark. I tried the door handle. It wasn't locked, so I gave it a twist.

I flipped on the light. The module was empty. His monitor and computer were shut down. His tools hung neatly on the wall. However, the mound of empty bean pods had grown considerably since last Friday.

Yet, I remained hopeful about Tobias's sudden vacation of the premises. Maybe he had gone to his cabin at last. I didn't take his flight personally. On the contrary, Tobias's own manic shyness caused him to retreat. Perhaps sharing a meal with his employer would be an unbearable anxiety for him. Regardless of the method, I was glad that I compelled him to go home to his cabin. I counted it a small step forward that he moved out of his lab module and into more suitable quarters at last. I noticed the mound of bean pods. Perhaps, his diet would improve as well.

Then I noticed something odd.

Tobias's gravipeds had been placed side by side on the seat of his console chair. Unweighted, he would have a devil of a time keeping his feet on the floor. The slightest exertion and he might go floating off. He must have had another pair with him. Perhaps, these were for the greenhouse alone. Yes, that would fit young Tobias. Shy and fastidious.

"John!"

I turned in the doorway of the lab module.

Jerry Willis, my master gardener, came bounding down the brick way. "John!" In his flight, he overshot me, but grabbed the aluminum soffit of the lab roof to stall his momentum. He pivoted on the corner, spinning around to face me as he drove his heavy peds down, planting them on the brick. After a bobble, he straightened. "You need to come to the park right away."

By the look on his face, I already knew the trouble. "Are the kids bouncing into the struts again?"

He shook his head, "It's the new man. What's his name? Hubert? Herbert? He's up on the ceiling. He won't come down. Something is wrong with him."

"Herman," I groaned softly, turned and bounded after Jerry back to the park area.

A crowd of children stood there, along with some parents and several of my staff. Their heads tipped back as they gazed at the ceiling of the arboretum.

Of course, Tobias was the object of their stares and murmurs. He floated spread-eagle, facing down at us as he gently bumped along the girder work along with the flotsam of leaves, blades of grass and twigs that the grounds people spent hours netting off the ceiling several times a week. He was high enough that I couldn't make out his expression, except that it seemed strangely neutral. Nor did he make any noise at all. He seemed stunned, just drifting around and thumping into girders without any effort to save himself.

"Did he touch the transformers?"

Jerry shrugged. "Don't know. The kids saw him first. They didn't see any sparks or hear anything. I guess he just floated into view."

It was bizarre to say the least. My suspicion that Tobias needed a close psychiatric evaluation was cemented, but first we had to get him down from there. "Has anyone called security?"

"They're coming."

I watched Tobias a moment longer. "Paramedics?"

"Also coming."

I sighed. Poor Tobias. I stepped into the middle of the crowd and cupped my hands around my mouth. "Tobias. Can you hear me?"

He never stirred, but slowly drifted against one of the curving I-beams that secured the ceiling. His shoulder snagged there.

"I think he's unconscious," Jerry said.

Somehow I knew that he wasn't. I knew that he was awake, aware and staring down at us from his vantage point. Perhaps he was more fragile than I realized and my polite ultimatum earlier in the day caused some sort of break down. "Tobias! Tobias Herman!"

He floated like a balloon. He stared like a doll.

The children gathered around me began to call out to him. Little voices shouted out, "Tobias. Tobias." Some full of helpful intent, while others were simply mocking. Before I could admonish them, other adults hushed their shouting. One of the older boys, a teen, stepped closer to me and, with an impulsive gleam in his eyes, suggested, "We could bounce up and pull him down with a rope."

"We'll wait for the paramedics." I told the boy. After all, they were trained for this sort of thing. Aside from protecting Tobias's welfare, the publicity was already bad enough to make the hairs stand up on the back of my neck. The last thing the arboretum needed was a bunch of adolescent boys bouncing around a ceiling full of transformers and lighting, throwing lassos at my stunned botanist in a crude rescue attempt.

The boy frowned and turned toward his friends, griping, "I told you he wouldn't let us do it." The little mob moved off grumbling.

Security and the rescue team arrived together. While security pushed the growing crowd back to the brick way, the paramedics wasted no time spreading their rigging on the lawn, set petons, then roped off and made a clean bounce toward the ceiling. Jerry and I watched while one of the paramedics climbed along the beams toward Tobias.

Jerry shook his head. "How'd he manage to get up there in the first place?"

"I found his gravipeds in his lab."

Jerry blinked at me. "He took them off?"

"Apparently."

"Why?"

The word just came to me. *Escape,* I thought, but I didn't say it. Tobias was deeply troubled. I saw that now. I swallowed a moment of pity. How desperate and deluded the poor fellow must be to flee my dinner invitation, to flee human comfort and human assistance in such a bizarre way. I couldn't fathom the depth of harm to his spirit. In spite of his troubles, I liked young Tobias Herman, so I was compelled to understand. I wanted to see him happy and well. I wanted to help him.

The paramedic reached Tobias at last and extended a hand to grab his arm. For the first time, Tobias roused from his apparent stupor and rolled gently out of reach like a sleeper turning over in bed.

The paramedic called to him, voice barely reaching my ears, "Mr. Herman, are you injured?"

Tobias did not answer, having rolled out of reach to drift facing down at us again.

"Mr. Herman, I'm going to put this line around your waist." The paramedic said, nimbly crawling upside down across the eye beams like a spider. "We'll pull you down."

In the faintest of replies, Tobias said, "I rather not ...."

"What did he say?" Jerry looked at me.

I suppose having heard the refrain over and over during the passed week I was familiar enough with it to have filled in the vowels between the crisper more easily heard consonants but I didn't answer Jerry. I kept watching the paramedic, mentally moving with him over the ceiling, inching closer to Tobias, wanting to bring him down safely.

The paramedic told him, "it's not safe up here. You'll have to come down now." At that he pushed faintly off the support and captured Tobias in his arms. The crowd around me gave a jubilant hoop. I noticed that Tobias didn't struggle at all. He was just as limp in the paramedic's arms as he had been bumping around the ceiling of the arboretum. Another rescue worker on the ground gently drew on the line attached to the medic's harness and pulled them both to the grass. They bounced lightly. The medic took care to make sure his body shielded Tobias from the easy impact in case he had injuries, but I already knew that whatever harm came to Tobias happened long before he ended up on the ceiling. His wounds were of a variety too complex for a paramedic to treat.

One of the older boys noticed Tobias's blank expression and muttered, "freak."

His friends giggled.

The boy caught my stare and blushed. He and his friends moved away.

Thankfully security moved in and pushed the crowd further back. I remained close to the paramedics while they flicked a penlight in Tobias's eyes and checked his body for injuries.

"Is he on any medications, Doctor Shepherd?"

"Not that I know of." I looked at him. "Tobias?"

He didn't look at me at all, but stared up at the ceiling of the arboretum as if he meant to passively will himself back to that distant place.

The paramedics lifted him onto a gurney and secured it to the platform of a little electric evac cart and drove away. They used no sirens, but the cherry flashed yellow.

Health Services was not far away, so I hurried for the transit rail and caught the next tram headed toward the annex.

Several hours of sitting on the cheap foam filled seats of the waiting room began to wear on my patience as well as my back when Doctor Daggett strolled out of the archway to the treatment center with a clipboard in her hand. She noticed me at once and came my way, smiling. "Hello, John."

"Joanne. Have you taken Tobias's case?"

She nodded.

That was a relief to me. Joanne volunteered in the perennial section of the arboretum garden. We had gotten to know each other. Tobias was in competent hands. "How is he?"

"Not particularly communicative. Can you tell me what happened?"

I recounted the passed week since his arrival with the culmination of the episode in the arboretum. Then I asked her, "do you know what's wrong with him?"

"For starters, he's dehydrated and malnourished. Has he been eating at all?"

"Just bush beans that I know of."

She made a note on his chart then told me, "he's also withdrawn, possibly disassociative. He might have had a psychotic break, but he's not violent or delusional." She looked over his chart. "For that matter the only resistance Toby Herman has shown so far is verbal." She looked at me. "Does he have any family?"

"I don't think so." He had left his next of kin information blank on his application.

She nodded. "Well, he's definitely staying over night for a full psych assessment."

"Do you think he'll be alright?"

"I'll know more tomorrow. I'll call you, John. And don't worry. We'll take good care of Toby."

"One thing, Joanne."

"What's that?"

"He's doesn't like to be called Toby. Tobias is better."

"Thanks," she said, making another note on the chart.

I went back to my cabin. Though Joanne told me not to worry, I did just a bit. Poor Tobias. He was such a mild soul that I had hunch the hospital full of human beings would be utter torture for him. But. It was all for the best. They would make him well.

Health Services kept Tobias only a few days. I visited him during that time, but only once. The truth is I hadn't the heart to go into his room. I felt guilty that he should be here at all, even though he needed to be. Watching him through the little window in the door of his room, it was quite clear to me that Tobias did not like being there though he sat impassively in his hospital bed with an IV taped to his hand. Occasionally, he looked over at the empty beds on either side of him. He never frowned. He never sighed. He simply sat, patiently enduring the tedium of his treatment. He looked thin and tired; a condition that seemed to as much a part of his soul as his body. It worried me. I couldn't believe there was anything but utter desperation behind those inscrutable brown eyes.

I met with Joanne shortly after in her office.

I perched on the edge of the chair before her desk as she told me, "I don't normally share patient information with anyone but immediate family members, but you're the only person who's stepped forward on Tobias's behalf, John, so...."

"That's quite alright, Joanne. I'd like to help him if I can."

She smiled. "That's good because we're releasing him this evening."

"So soon?"

"I've diagnosed him as having Social Anxiety Disorder. Do you know what that is?

"Well...."

"Essentially it's a fear of social situations and interaction with other people. Tobias has a rather severe case. I think the stress of the new job, coming to the sphere, meeting and dealing with so many new people was simply too much for him. He suffered a mild psychotic break that triggered a fugue episode."

"You mean what happened in the Arboretum with him floating on the ceiling?"

Joanne nodded.

"What do we do?"

"I've given him a prescription to help relieve any symptoms of anxiety he may be having and scheduled some sessions. Other than that there isn't much we can do. It's really up to Tobias. My primary concern is that he's withdrawn and noncommunicative."

"I've noticed that he seems, well, terribly shy."

She nodded, smiling in sympathy. "That could simply be part of the SAD pathology. For some patients the sheer anxiety of being around other people triggers mutism." She looked me carefully in the eyes. "Honestly, John, I'm not sure he's up to remaining here. We may have to think in terms of building documentation to have Tobias returned to the moon, maybe all the way back to Earth."

"But his life's work has been in low G food production. What in God's name would he do if we ship him back to Earth? His career will be ruined. Joanne, the boy has a genius for exoterran agriculture."

"I'm not saying he has to go now. I'm just saying that he needs to be watched and guided."

I sighed. In spite of my affection for Tobias, I was a little ambivalent about the task. He had been a handful since I met him only a week and a half ago. I wondered a moment whether I had built false expectations, believing in the promise of the botanical engineering miracles he could work in my department rather than seeing the reality. Yet, the truth remained. Those were his root mats holding the lawns and flowerbeds firmly to the floor of the arboretum. One day, because of his invention, fields of grass and billowing flowers would fill both bowls of the sphere from rim to rim. That gift alone stalled my doubts. There was good reason to keep hoping. "The medication will help him?"

"It usually does in cases like this."

"Very well then. What do you want me to do?"

As Joanne instructed, I escorted Tobias to the pharmacist to pick up his pills, then walked him to his cabin in the residence module. We passed through the check-in at the front desk. As always Tobias was quietly compliant, signing in at the clerk's request without the least flicker of resentment which left me with a faint feeling of guilt. I knew that deep down this was not what Tobias wanted at all. He wanted his lab module, his bed of fertilizer sacks and bush beans. He wanted the inertia and solitude of that place.

At his door, he tapped the thumb lock and let us inside.

The lights came up softly. The cabin was freshly painted, done in neutral shades of white and beige. Of course, it was furnished with gravity assist furniture. "This is a nice place, Tobias. More comfortable than the lab module, don't you think?"

Without answering Tobias's gaze wandered over his surroundings. His expression remained uncertain. Though he clutched the plastic bag with his medication in his hand, it looked forgotten. He reminded me of a child who lost his mother in the crowd and was too stunned to wail. I touched his shoulder. "You'll be fine here. And don't forget that you have my number. Call me if you need anything." I went to the door and turned back once more. Tobias still stood there, holding his bag and staring at the wall. "I'll see you at work in the morning then. Alright?"

"Yes, Sir," he said softly.

As I left him, I suffered the awful premonition that he would stand there all night, staring at the wall, holding that damned plastic bag, caught up in that strange mood of inertia that seemed to be slowly consuming him.

Come morning, I no sooner sat down at my desk when the com buzzed.

Jerry appeared on my walltall, frowning, "John, that nutcase is at it again."

Of course, I knew at once who the 'nutcase' was and what he was 'at' again. The odd thing was that I was relieved that Tobias came to the arboretum this morning and wasn't still standing in his cabin, staring at the wall. "Where is he?"

"Guess."

"Not floating."

"Floating." Jerry's frown deepened. "Should I call security?"

I can't describe the sick feeling it gave me, but I nodded.

They pulled Tobias down and hauled him away to Health Services once more. Like before Tobias didn't put up a fight. Though his eyes were glassy, lined and gray from lack of sleep, his thin face was full of placid resolve. Tobias no longer cared what we did to him. He functioned on instinct now, returning to the arboretum for him was like a salmon laddering upstream to its spawning grounds. He sought to quell the urge to free float, to look down on us all from that quiet, drifting place, unfettered and peaceful.

It gave me a chill.

This time Joanne committed him. She insisted that I let her take over for a while. I confess I was relieved. Overwhelmed and feeling inadequate to help Tobias at all, I was ready to let the professionals cocoon him in their attention. I hoped that he might reappear bright eyed and smiling in the door of the arboretum one day soon; malaise wiped from his demeanor by his medication and plenty of attentive therapy. I wanted to see Tobias again, but I wanted to see him happy.

For a week, then two, I managed to put Tobias out of my mind. With one less botanist, the workload in the arboretum increased. Though I should have split Tobias's responsibilities among the rest of the staff, I took on his research schedule personally. It let me turn my whole attention to transplanting and rotating crops, keeping all of the new nets growing, harvesting and documenting the test groups. It gave me the opportunity to help young Tobias in some small way so that when he was well enough to come back to his green house, he wouldn't be overwhelmed with a backlog of work.

Joanne's nurse called one afternoon, asking me if I would like to see him. I agreed at once, hoping to see some progress. We set up a time. That evening I headed off to Health Services with a bag of bush beans for him as sort of a private joke between us.

As I passed the nurses' station, I stopped to ask them where Tobias was. They looked at each other oddly and told me, "the day room."

Following the signs, I found the wide, bright room. There at the back, away from a couple of patients sliding checkers around a slotted board built into one of the games tables, Tobias sat, secured in a weighted wheel chair alone at a window that faced the arboretum. I was shocked to see that he required a wheel chair then noticed the IV bag drifting on one of the metal rings on the back of his chair. His arms were desperately thin.

One of the nurses at the desk appeared beside me in the doorway. "He's been refusing food since he was admitted."

I looked at the bag of bush beans in my hand.

"For him?" she asked.

I nodded, ignoring the flush of embarrassment that warmed my face.

"I don't think he'll be able to swallow those," she said.

"No one told me." I said, stunned. "Why didn't anyone tell me?"

"We've been working with him intensely."

That was probably the worse thing for Tobias. He loved his solitude. He needed it. All these people fluttering around him, prodding at him and asking him endless questions almost certainly mortified his shy spirit. No doubt it all forced him to retreat deeper and deeper into himself. "But the medication?"

She shrugged. "I don't know what to tell you." Her lashes drooped as she looked at the back of Tobias's head. "Sometimes they just don't respond. It's a matter of will. He's been resisting us from the very beginning."

I watched him, feeling as though I had been nailed to the floor. I realized, "No, he began resisting long before that."

She blinked at me.

"Can I ...."

"Of course. Doctor Daggett hopes your visit would stimulate him."

Hesitant now, I crossed the room to Tobias's chair. The guilt alone weighed so heavily on my heart that I was sure I could slip off my gravipeds without chancing the slightest drift. Still, I turned up a bright smile as I came to the back of his chair. "Hello, Tobias. I hear you've been having a rough time."

As usual, he had nothing to say. The air around him was still. I noticed that he stared at the arboretum. My heart tore a little. Even now, quietly trying to starve himself to death, he longed to return to the arboretum. "That's all you want, isn't it?" Maybe I had been too forceful, making him leave the lab module, making him go to his cabin. He really hadn't done anything offensive except refuse to conform to my expectations. He hadn't harmed a soul. We - no, I should have just left him alone. Let him have the lab module. What did it matter? I placed the baggie of bush beans in his lap. "I thought you might like these."

His bony hands remained on the armrests of his chair.

All I had to do was leave him alone. He might have been all right. None this would have happened. None of it had to happen. I confessed, "I'm sorry, Tobias."

He remained terribly still.

"Did you hear me? I said that I'm sorry."

Still nothing.

"Tobias," I said, "Tobias, what if I promise that you could go back to the lab module. What if I promise that you could stay there. Live there. Whatever you want. But you must start eating again. You must."

Just then his right hand slowly rose from the arm of his chair. At first, I thought he was reaching for the bag of bush beans. I thought it was a miracle. I hit upon his deepest desire and stirred it. But what I thought was awakening spirit turned out to be escaping spirit.

Tobias's scrawny right hand continued to rise. Then the left one followed. His head bobbled like a balloon on a stick. His dimmed gaze locked on the arboretum dome. I stammered, "nurse," over my shoulder.

She came quickly, touched his wrist then turned to another nurse just arriving in the day room. "Call a code."

Of course, they were much too late.

No relatives came to claim Tobias so I did. I made his arrangements and eventually brought the urn with his ashes back to the arboretum where I placed it in the hollow of a memorial obelisk. It bore his name and his contribution to our little Eden. Without Tobias C. Herman, Stuart Roosa Arboretum would never have become the green solace that it is to so many.

After the ceremony the others, mostly my staff and several loyal patrons of the arboretum, drifted away after an hour or so. They offered me kind wishes and encouragement for my efforts to save young Tobias. Jerry patted my shoulder and told me, "You were a good friend to him, John." Although I'm not confident Tobias would have thought so. I tried to be one to him just the same.

I lingered a while, gazed at the engraving on the lean, white obelisk and listened to the quiet enfold me as the grow lights in the ceiling dimmed. I could nearly feel Tobias there, drifting in the arboretum dusk high above the curly limbs of the trees and shrubs. The sound of solitude crept into me by degrees. I wondered if this was what Tobias felt when he was alone and undoubtedly most content. Without people, without the constant of clatter voices and clashing egos a pleasant stillness filled me. I looked up half expecting to catch Tobias up there, floating, maybe even smiling for a change.

Of course, the ceiling was empty of anything but darkness and struts.

What was it Tobias saw from up there? Was he simply comforted by the distance from other human beings? Was it the perspective of height? Was he admiring the fine little oasis his root mats created in the sphere? I looked up again. Perhaps, he wanted one last look before .... I shook off the thought.

Then I looked up again. Or, maybe it was so. I realized. Tobias didn't come to live in sphere. He came to die here. He told me that he came for the gravity, but he didn't come to conquer the lack of it, only accept it. He wanted the privilege to float, to practice death before he embraced it completely.

That strange, shy, little brown eyed man breathed out his one note of genius; to bedeck the sterile gray canvas of sphere's bowl with Earth's most precious jewels then he bowed gently into the dark, asking for no honors or nods of acknowledgement. He only wanted a quiet moment to admire what he made.

At least, that's what I suspected, but I had an inkling that the real answer waited for me up there. If nothing else I would pay homage to my

diffident friend's one great masterwork. So I
slipped off my gravipeds and pushed off.

If you ever come to the Stuart Roosa
Arboretum, may I suggest you do the same.

www.ingramcontent.com/pod-product-compliance
Lightning Source LLC
Chambersburg PA
CBHW070613130626
46556CB00001B/354